SOUTH OF THE GILA

South of the Gila

BOB CASEMORE

A Black Horse Western

ROBERT HALE · LONDON

ISBN 0 7090 5917 5

Robert Hale Limited
Clerkenwell House
Clerkenwell Green
London EC1R 0HT

For Rosemarie

*The characters and events in this book
are fictitious. Any resemblance to persons
living or dead is purely coincidental.*

Photoset in North Wales by
Derek Doyle & Associates, Mold, Clwyd.
Printed and bound in Great Britain by
WBC Book Manufacturers Limited,
Bridgend, Mid-Glamorgan.

ONE

Neil McAdam, riding his mustang Dixie, grinned as he considered the good news he'd tell Zack Meadows, his foreman. The grin vanished as a lone rider galloped toward him out of the night.

'Neil! You'd best get your ass over to the Sagebrush pronto!' the rider yelled. 'They bushwhacked Meadows and Vanderman!'

Neil recognized the voice of Harry Hawthorne before he got a clear view of the owner of the Hawthorne mine. He reined in Dixie.

'They're roughing up your foreman and his assistant pretty bad. If you – someone – don't stop them sons of bitches you'll have to bury Zack and Ken afore sundown tomorrow.'

'Whoa, friend!' Neil's soft southern drawl hardened. 'What sons of bitches?'

'Don't know, three of 'em wearing masks.'

Neil's thoughts raced with the pace of his mustang as he and Hawthorne headed toward Apache Bend, settled over the mother lode in this southern area of Arizona territory. He'd been savoring the good news he planned to tell Zack Meadows, his young Kansan crew chief at the Benson mine.

For the first time in over a year there'd been a profitable haul of silver from Merle Benson's mine.

5

He'd promised Miss Benson that he'd put the mine 'back on its feet', and he'd done so.

Now his good news was blunted by Hawthorne's bad tidings. Neil set his jaw. Already there'd been too much unexplained trouble at the string of mines extending north and south from Apache Bend.

Five minutes later, Neil leaped from Dixie then tethered him to the rail outside the Sagebrush. Followed by Hawthorne, and with his revolver ready for action, he burst through the swinging doors of the Sagebrush.

'What the hell's going on here?' he shouted.

The silver miners present and some of the girls from the rooms upstairs had moved to the sides of the room. They faced the Winchester rifles brandished by two of the masked assailants, men who were short and heavy set. The third masked man, tall, slim, raw-boned, stood over the prostrate Zack Meadows. He ground his boot into the shoulder of the Kansan. Zack yelled in pain and rage. He struggled to get up but his assailant held him back.

Neil's quick sizing up of Zack's plight also took in Ken's. Vanderman, on his knees by the brass rail on the bar, his face bloodied, stared at several of his teeth that had changed their location in his mouth to the palm of his left hand. His right arm hung motionless at his side.

Neil fired a shot toward the smoke-smudged ceiling. It put out a kerosene lamp, one of a circle of such lamps mounted around the rim of a wagon wheel.

'What the devil's going on?' he yelled again, as if his ears needed to hear what his eyes saw.

The shot and his second shout compelled the two

with rifles to turn and face Neil. At Neil's command, their rifles clattered to the sawdust covered floor.

Neil put a slug alongside the boot of the tall stranger. The man lifted his other boot from Zack's face. He wheeled to face McAdam. Neil noted the tall man's rifle stood against the bar.

'Take it easy, Mister,' the assailant said. 'Best you keep outta something don't concern you nohow.' He turned back to the prone Meadows. 'You had enough, smart boy?' This time he pounded his spurred boot into the hapless foreman's leg. The sharp-pointed rowel ripped through Zack's pants. It tore into the flesh of his calf and thigh. Zack groaned. The stranger continued. 'Lucky your boss McAdam ain't around. I'd give him a dose of the same treatment.' He lifted his boot from Zack's leg. 'We'll run McAdam right outta the territory.'

Neil raised his voice. 'Now's your chance – whoever you are – hiding behind that fucking mask. I ain't wearing one. Tell him who I am, men.'

Eddie Cox, the bartender and owner of the Sagebrush raised his head from behind the long bar.

'He's Neil McAdam, stranger.'

'I've been introduced,' Neil said with menacing calm. 'Now who the hell are you?'

'Ain't got to answer no questions, smart boy.'

'Outta the territory, eh?' McAdam said. 'Ready to start me on my way?' He put another slug at the feet of the two stocky riflemen. They raised their hands above their heads.

The tall man edged away from the hurt Meadows. 'Like I said, McAdam, take it easy.' He moved to retrieve his rifle that leaned against the bar.

'Leave it!' Neil commanded.

'We ain't armed – now, McAdam.'

'I don't hold to killing,' Neil said. A note of sadness crept into his voice. Neil handed his .44 to Hawthorne. 'I'm not armed either.' Fists raised, Neil advanced on the stranger who backed to the bar. Then the masked man lunged at his challenger. Neil dodged one way, feinted the other, and then let fly a sharp, bone-crushing uppercut. He connected with the man's jaw. The brute's head snapped backward. Neil followed the uppercut with a right cross to the left eye behind the mask. Then he let loose with a left to the bruiser's nose. A sudden spurt of red came on the heel of the blow. The man howled, then joined his two companions.

The three strangers, hands stretched toward the ceiling, each keeping a wary eye on Neil, backed out the doors. A moment later Neil heard them curse as they mounted their horses, then rode off.

One of the miners spoke up. 'I seen what they did to Ken, Neil. One of them short fellahs pinned your crewman's arms behind his back.' He looked at Vanderman who nodded his corroboration. 'Then the other shortie pounded his fist in Ken's belly and then in his face. Two or three times, maybe more. Then the bastard brought his knee up into the poor guy's balls.'

Neil glared at the gathering. 'What have we got here? Fifteen, twenty of you men? And you never raised a hand to help my foreman? Some of you've got six-shooters. Scared to use them?'

'Easy, Neil,' Hawthorne advised. 'We've all got enough trouble at our mines as it is. It's got a lot of the fellahs cowed.'

Neil, his temper cooling, nodded. He stared at

Zack and Ken. Had his men been roughed up so they couldn't work for awhile? Was somebody out to mess up production at Miss Benson's mine, now that it showed a profit? Who?

'I can't walk, Neil,' Zack whispered, 'and Ken's got a wing that won't fly.'

'Harry, will you help me get my men over to Doc Whitman's?' Neil asked. 'I'd be obliged for sure.'

Fifteen minutes later, Zack and Ken were in Doc's home.

Half the people in Apache Bend, Arizona Territory, didn't know that he'd been christened William Whitman some 60 years ago in Tennessee; they only knew him as Doc and he had never asked for a fancier handle. Tonight, the short, white-haired doctor, rough surgeon and undertaker, seemed more tired than usual. Still, after plying Zack and Ken with bourbon to ease the pain, he worked with deft and steady hands, plus Neil's help, in setting the broken bones.

Guy Rengert, the county sheriff, came into Doc Whitman's office. His cold, slate eyes, deep-set under a balding pate, stared at the doc's handiwork and then turned to Neil.

'Your men, McAdam?'

'If you mean they're on Miss Benson's payroll, I reckon you're right.'

'Who roughed them up?'

'You tell me, sheriff.'

'I figger they's strangers. Talked to Eddie Cox and some of the miners and they said they ain't seen them afore. Can't keep an eye on everyone. Place is growing.'

'What are you going to do about it, Guy?' Doc

Whitman asked. He always ignored Sheriff Rengert's star.

'Can't do much. Mebbe nothing. Seems like they's just some wild boys passing through, liquored up, spoiling for a fight. Nobody kilt anyways, but I'll keep my eyes open.'

'Meanwhile do me a favor, Guy,' Doc said. 'Stop off on your way back and have Dolly Meadows and Betsy Vanderman come by with buggies to fetch their men home.'

Sheriff Rengert nodded, then turned to Neil. 'Sorry about what happened, McAdam.'

'Hope you mean you're sorry you're too late to arrest those sidewinders. Seems like you're always a mite late to have your gun and a set of handcuffs ready, sheriff.'

Without replying to Neil's rebuff, Rengert stalked out and rode off.

'You're a mite late yourself, Doc.' Neil's grin was wide as the big canyon of the Colorado River. 'Today's June 14th.'

'Sure and it's Saturday. Tomorrow's Sunday. You daft?'

'You ain't changed that calendar page on your wall since last June, the one with Grant's picture on it. We've come a year away now from summer of eighteen and seventy-two.'

Doc Whitman nodded. 'Don't aim to change it. That's the month my Martha died. Tribute to her.' Then he eyed Neil. 'I see you name our president with some bitterness. Never mind, I'll ask no questions. Reminds me though of a time when I was a young buck serving with Sam Houston in 'thirty-six. We were facing Santa Anna at San Jacinto in April at the time.'

'Please, Doc, no stories. I've got too many worries at the mine.'

Doc Whitman nodded. He never took offence. He lit his pipe and kept watch on the two Benson employees. Shortly, there was the sound of horses and buggy wheels outside. Doc and Neil helped get Zack and Ken to the buggies and commended them to the care of their wives. Doc gave a few instructions to Dolly and Betsy and slipped them some powders to help their husbands sleep.

Back in his office, Doc turned a tired attention again to Neil. 'I'm sorry to see this happen to Merle,' he said. 'Knew her since she was in pigtails. Nobody had a better friend than I had in her daddy. Now, there's all this trouble.'

'Started at the Benson mine,' Neil said. His blue eyes darkened. 'After Tom Benson died I stayed on 'cause Miss Benson asked me to manage things for her.'

'That's because you had a lot of experience, boy.'

'You've got that right.' Neil mused. Yes, he had a lot of experience. In silver mines in Mexico, then in New Mexico, Arizona and Colorado territories. A year at one mine, two years at another. Always moving, running for eight long years since that day in '65. He shook himself free of his thoughts.

'There's been a lot of accidents, Neil. Leastways they call them accidents. I've done some patching up, I'll tell you.'

'I know. That explosion at Hawthorne's mine shut down his operation for a while. Felkins found a dynamite bomb in his shaft, but he defused it in time. Some of Olsen's men are quitting because they're scared about what's happening.'

'You can bet Harry Hawthorne and Matt Felkins

won't ever walk away from trouble. Not those old Indian fighters.'

'Reckon you're right, Doc.'

'And neither would Tom Benson.'

'Seems that's when all this started, that cave-in at Benson's where Tom was killed. It was a cave-in all right, but it wasn't natural.' Again he shook off the idea.

Doc's gaze was steady, level, shrewd, when he next spoke. 'Funny, though, nothing seems to happen to the Gila operation.'

Neil nodded. 'Caleb Dunne's sure lucky. Anyway, he's had trouble enough since he took control of the Gila after his brother's death.' Neil shook his head. The murder of Howard Dunne still kept everyone's tongue busy in Apache Bend, as had the flight of young Joel Dunne, Howard's son. Caleb Dunne had accused his nephew of the crime. 'You believe Joel did it, Doc?'

'Probably. I expect the kid's clean to Canada by now.'

Neil thanked Doc Whitman, told the tired medic that Miss Benson would take care of all expenses for Zack and Ken, and then left.

He mounted his mustang and headed for Merle Benson's house to tell her the news.

'Come on, Dixie!' No one in Apache Bend had asked him why he named his horse Dixie. Unlike folks in Georgia, no one in the West ever asked about your past. What a man was *now* was all that counted.

He trotted through the town. He had come to love it, with its dusty main street, its wooden sidewalks, the blacksmith's forge, the Wells Fargo bank, the

general store and post office. He rode past the
Tumbleweed Hotel and stage stop, and on beyond
the little church and the picket-fenced cemetery
with its wood markers. He had been a stranger and
Apache Bend had welcomed him.

More importantly, Tom Benson had given him a
job in his silver mine, one of six such mines near
the town, a mother lode stretching south to north.
Benson's mine was at the southern end of the
string, Caleb Dunne's Gila mine at the northern
end.

More than ever, Neil felt a deep responsibility to
Merle Benson. When her father lost his life, she
had turned to Neil to help her. She had asked him
to be her manager. More than that, she had
offered him a share in the mine – 35 percent of the
profits if he could keep it going. He swore that he
would.

His troubled thoughts so occupied him that he
was unaware that Dixie had carried him past the
Benson mine office, where he slept by choice for
the time being. Ten minutes later he came to Merle
Benson's house, a small, comfortable, adobe
structure.

He knew it would be hard to break the news to
her of the fight at the Sagebrush. She had
approved of the two men he had hired. She would
do everything she could to help their wives while
the men were out of work.

The mid-June night was cool. Merle Benson had
opened the windows of her parlor. The pretty
curtains she had made fluttered in the evening
breeze. Neil could hear the soft notes of *Old Folks at
Home*. He could see her petite figure at her
heirloom pianoforte as she played. Her brown

curls shone in the lamplight.

He knocked. She smiled when she opened the door. Then her smile changed to a worried frown.

'Oh, my God, Neil, what's happened?'

TWO

Merle Benson urged him to come in.

He removed his hat. Always the sight of her stirred him. He told her of the brawl at the Sagebrush.

'I didn't want no killing. I backed those three off, but they'd done their harm. They lit out real fast, Miss Benson.'

Merle shuddered as she listened to his account. 'Before you tell me more,' she said, 'I'll make fresh coffee. I baked some buttermilk biscuits this afternoon and I'll warm them. I've a new honeycomb I took from the skep I queened a month ago.'

Seated in the kitchen, he watched her warm the biscuits in the oven of her wood-burning range. Just being with her warmed him, too. She ground coffee beans. She brought a pot of water to boil and added the ground coffee. The aroma of biscuits and coffee filled the room.

'I suspect someone thinks you'll be easy to force out because you're a woman. You can count on me to see that it doesn't happen, Miss Benson.'

Despite her worries, she smiled. 'Miss Benson? Isn't it about time you called me Merle? Maybe you felt you couldn't when dad was alive, but you can now.'

He returned the smile. In all his twenty-six years, Merle Benson was the prettiest girl he'd ever seen. 'I'm not sure it's the proper thing to do, Miss Benson, but I'll think on it.' He finished his coffee. 'Best I head back to the mine office. I'll keep my eyes peeled.'

'You'll come for supper tomorrow?'

'Reckon maybe I ought to ride into town and take my meals at the Tumbleweed.'

He said goodnight and added, 'Don't worry' in a voice he tried to make convincing as he left the kitchen and went outside. He stepped into the saddle. He spun the mustang around so he could face Merle who stood on the porch.

'Reckon I might change my mind. What are you having for supper tomorrow?'

'Ham from dad's mesquite smokehouse,' she said. 'Fried potatoes, string beans, Indian pudding, coffee.'

'I'll be there. Would you play me a song or two?'

'Three or four if you can stand it, Neil.'

'I'm sure partial, Miss Benson, to that piece, *Jeanie With the Light Brown Hair*.'

He tipped his broad-brimmed hat, used his knees to spur Dixie and trotted back toward the mine.

He eyed the millions of stars that seemed so close he could stand in the stirrups and touch them. The half-moon had not yet climbed up to do so. Beneath him was the sandy carpet of the high country, dotted here and there with jack pines and sage brush. The air was sweet with the blossoms of the saguaro cacti. To the west and south he could see the silhouettes of jagged mountain ranges.

Merle Benson's house was two miles from the

Benson diggings, a short canter for Dixie. The office was 50 yards from the mine itself. The layout was the same pattern as the other five diggings that stretched to the north and south of Apache Bend. Benson's had a main tunnel that sloped toward the hard rock subterrain. Narrow tracks ran the length of the tunnel so that small ore cars could be brought to the surface.

The main tunnel led to and passed by a number of shafts in which buckets filled with ore could be raised and empty ones lowered to be filled again. The shafts could be descended by ladders, and at various levels other tunnels branched out.

Six silver mines at Apache Bend all pretty much the same, except for Caleb Dunne's Gila which was slightly larger. Six digs, all busy ant hills crawling with industrious silver miners. Busy until recently, Neil knew, when incidents, maybe *accidents*, had stopped production at Hawthorne's, and threatened serious and costly shutdowns at others.

'For sure,' Neil muttered, 'Tom Benson's death was no accident.' Benson had worked that mine for 15 years, coming to Apache Bend after selling everything he owned back east in order to buy it. There had never been a cave-in at his digs before. Cave-ins happened, but none of the other mines had had one either. 'You know it was no accident, eh, Dixie boy?' Neil said as he rode up and dismounted at the Benson office.

It was a small, unpretentious adobe building serving as headquarters, with two windows, a plank door, a plank table, a desk, several chairs, and a Franklin stove that Benson brought from Montpelier in '58. To those meagre furnishings, Neil had added a cot, bedroll, a small stand with wash basin and pitcher. Above this hung an army issue mirror. At the rear of the office was a lean-to for stabling Dixie.

Of a sudden Neil had an uneasy feeling he was being watched as he removed the mustang's bridle, bit and reins; unfastened the surcingle, then hung up Dixie's saddle and stirrups.

Neil went into the office and lit a kerosene lamp. While he undressed he still harbored the uneasy feeling that he was being observed, that every move he made was noticed and studied. He decided it was because of the fight at the saloon, or from the way he'd been worrying about the mines. Was someone outside?

Neil extinguished the office lamp. Then he redressed himself quickly, slipped into mocassins as he had seen Tom Benson do so many times; took an unlit kerosene lantern then let himself out the adobe office with a sound as soft as a breeze coaxing tumbleweed over the desert.

He walked with panther tread to the mine entrance. Once a few yards inside, he lit the lantern. He moved down the tunnel staying to the center of the tracks. Now and then he paused to listen but he heard nothing other than the scampering of a desert rat. At other times, he glanced behind him but saw nothing except the shadows cast by the lantern. An uneasiness dogged his footsteps and with just as soft a tread.

He reached the main shaft. He descended some 30 feet to a level where smaller tunnels sloped away, one to his left and one to his right. Everything seemed in order. He looked for dynamite sticks, blasting caps and fuses, but found none. It was at this level, where he stood, that the cave-in had occurred, where Merle's father lost his life. He heard the rustling and saw the scurrying of vinegaroons, the dreaded venomous whip scorpions. They shied away from him; the lighted lantern made them keep their distance.

All was quiet. the buckets hung idle as they did each night because Miss Benson could not afford to put on more miners for an extra shift. The ore cars stood waiting on their rails in the two smaller tunnels. He ascended to the main tunnel. He moved cautiously along its length toward the thin moonlight ahead. He blew out the lantern when he came to the entrance. Silence. He paused at the entrance. Tom Benson's digs. Tom Benson who believed in him and whose daughter believed in him and trusted him as well. He sighed. Would the day come when he'd dare to call her Merle?

Perhaps not, but that wouldn't lessen his resolve to keep the mine going, whatever threat to himself. If he had to take a pickaxe to the rock himself, he'd do so. If he had to haul up buckets of ore, he would. He'd gladly take his place beside a mule if need be in order to pull the ore cars along the fucking tracks.

For sure, he'd work long hours for the Benson mine. He'd give his oath on it. He emerged from the mine and headed for the office.

Then Dixie alerted him to danger.

Neil heard the horse's neigh, loud and frantic, a high-pitched, full-throated cry of alarm.

Neil spun around, peering in every direction. The rising moon cast deeper shadows in the surrounding darkness. He started to run toward the office.

Then came the sharp report of a rifle. The bullet

tore into his left arm flesh and muscle high up on his bicep, searing it as with a knife made white hot in blacksmith Homer Breithalter's forge. Neil let loose a scream of pain and anger as he fell.

He lay in the dirt and sand near the entrance of the mine. He felt warm blood as it soaked his shirt. From miles away he heard the frenzied neighing of Dixie. He looked up. He hurt but he was all right. The million stars of an earlier hour were still there.

THREE

Neil heard the sound of rapid hoofbeats, but he wasn't sure if the horse and rider were leaving the mine area or coming toward him. Was the rifleman returning to finish his cowardly deed?

Shortly, the unknown rider halted his horse and dismounted a few yards away from Neil. He blocked out the view of the stars as he bent over the wounded Benson manager.

'That you, McAdam? You all right?'

'Yes and no. I'm alive. Got winged though by someone. You Brad Connors?'

'Sure as hell am.'

'Recognized your voice. Sure hope it wasn't you, Brad, using me for target practice.'

'You know I wouldn't shoot a man without giving him time to draw. Anyways, too dark to draw a bead on anyone. I heard a shot though, and thought I'd better check.'

Brad Connors owned the silver mine just north of Matt Felkins' digs. Neil knew that Connors was having a struggle to keep his operation going. He was working with a short crew. Connors was a man of fifty, graying, with tired eyes and bowed shoulders. He had never married. Neil had heard that silver was the only wife Connors wanted.

'You strong enough to walk over to your office? Maybe I can sling you over Ginger's saddle.' Connor's roan mare snorted.

'I'll walk. I can make it if I can lean on you, Brad.'

'Do the best I can with my game leg.'

Neil stood and shook his head to clear it of a momentary dizziness. His left arm felt as if some cowpuncher's branding iron had left its mark on his bicep. Brad Connors half-supported him as they moved slowly across the 50 yards to the office.

Neil knew it had to be a chore for Brad to help him walk. Struggle, hardship and a leg crippled during a cattle stampede years ago, had aged him a score of years beyond his own.

Once inside, Neil stretched out on his cot. Brad lit a lamp and then loosened Neil's shirt. Dried blood glued the sleeve to Neil's upper arm and shoulder.

'I'll fetch Doc Whitman,' Brad said.

As Connors was about to leave, Neil spoke. 'Any trouble at your digs, Brad?'

'Not yet, but I hear there's plenty brewing. Tennant'll take care of any if it comes.'

Grant Tennant was Brad's foreman and Neil knew Tennant could be provoked easily into a fight.

'Tell him to watch things, Brad. There's something fishy going on.'

Connors nodded and limped out. Neil heard the roan, Ginger, head toward Apache Bend at a gallop.

A half hour later, Doc Whitman cut away Neil's sleeve. Then he helped Neil remove his shirt, muttering the while. 'Won't let me get a night's sleep, will you?' He tossed the bloodied shirt and its separated sleeve aside. 'Nice shirt.'

'Doc, stop the chatter and get to work.'

'Won't be pleasant, son. I'm out of anaesthetic. Ordered chloroform from St. Joseph. Due in next week. Want a man-size slug of bourbon?'

'Yep, doc. Sure could use it.' He took four deep swallows from the bottle Whitman handed him.

'Brad, you hold the lamp so I can see what the devil I'm doing,' Doc ordered. Then, he took a dressing from his bag, rolled it into a tight mass in the shape and thickness of two fingers. He told Neil to open his mouth. 'Here, bite down on this.'

'What for?'

'Shit, so you don't chew off your tongue.' He winked at Connors. 'We don't want to hear you howl like a wounded coyote. Hold him down, Brad.' Doc Whitman probed the wound in Neil's upper arm, searching, feeling, drawing blood. Sweat broke out on Neil's forehead and upper lip.

'Relax, Neil, don't fight me. Bullet's in there, lodged against the bone. Distance probably saved you from too much damage.' Doc whistled. 'Whoever it was had good aim. Aha, here we are!'

Neil sighed and spat out the rolled up dressing.

'Now, this'll sting, Neil. I'll just pour some of this bourbon onto your wound. Best disinfectant west of the Mississippi.'

Doc dressed the wound. 'Better settle in for a couple of days, give it a chance to heal.' He bent over the table and examined the bullet. 'You got a souvenir, son. .50 caliber, maybe .52, can't always tell the difference.' He looked up. 'Can't tell from a slug alone what kind of weapon shot it.'

Neil shook his head. 'Carbine maybe?'

'Maybe not.' He turned to leave. 'You shouldn't be alone.'

'I'm okay.'

Doc sighed. 'You'll need that dressing changed. There's the risk of infection.'

'I know.' Neil regarded Connors. 'Brad, it's a lot to ask, but would you get Miss Benson to come around in the morning? Not tonight, mind you, but tomorrow.'

Early the next morning Merle Benson arrived at the office on her palomino, Firefly. She brought a basket of fruit, bread, butter, strawberry jam, and a jar full of coffee, still warm. Her pretty face was taut with worry, a concern mixed with mock anger.

'Mr. Connors told me what happened. Neil, I won't allow you to stay here. You need attention. It's not safe.'

'I'm not one to hide behind a lady's skirts, Miss Benson. Besides, I've got to be on hand at the mine. Zack and Ken can't be here. I'll take Zack's place.'

After he had eaten, Merle changed Neil's dressing. She felt his forehead. 'You're very warm. Are you all right?'

'Reckon a little fever goes hand in hand with a bullet.'

'You'll stay here, resting, at least today and tomorrow.'

'You're forgetting I'm to show myself for supper.'

'It will wait.'

Merle Benson left. Through the window he saw her mount Firefly and ride off.

On Monday morning, despite his promise to his boss, Neil walked carefully to the Benson mine. Ore cars were coming to the surface, their contents to be dumped into heavy wagons drawn by mules. He paused for a moment to clear his head.

Two men standing at the mouth of the mine welcomed him and voiced their feelings about someone who would bushwhack a man in the dark.

'Oughta do what we do to an ornery horse,' one miner said.

'Thanks, men, but we don't want a two-legged gelding running loose in Arizona.'

An hour later, Merle Benson came into Sheriff Rengert's adobe office at the north end of Apache Bend. Her chin was a little higher than usual, her brown eyes were not merry. They showed determination worthy of any man. She spoke with level tones that barely concealed her anger.

'Sheriff Rengert, I want to report a shooting on my property.'

Guy Rengert took his spurred boots off his desk, straightened up, checked his star. He didn't remove his hat. 'You don't say.'

'Someone shot my manager – at my mine.'

'You don't say, ma'am. I seen McAdam this past Saturday night. Is he – is he dead?'

'Of course not. He's wounded.'

'Well I'm right pleased to hear he's alive.'

'It's just another blow to the mine operation.'

'I sure feel sorry about that, ma'am. Your daddy and all, and those two hands of yours getting themselves into a fight.'

'Sheriff, I've got a mine to run, and a profit to make. What are you going to do about what's happening?'

'Well, I plan to investigate, part of my job, even if I ain't got nothing to go on. Now, you just go back to your mine and don't worry them pretty curls of yours.'

Merle left his office with her chin even higher than when she went in.

That Monday afternoon at the mine, one of the men tapped Neil on his good shoulder and told him someone wanted to see him at the mine entrance.

Neil was at the second level tunnel, where ore was being raised by hand in the buckets. They rattled their way up the shaft to the main tunnel as Neil climbed the ladder alongside them. He could grasp the crude rings with his right hand only. It was a slow climb. Neil took nearly three times as long to reach the top than previously when he scampered up. The pain in his left arm was a reminder of Merle's caution to stay in the office, to rest, to heal.

Caleb Dunne stood near the mine entrance. His chestnut stallion was nearby. As Neil emerged into the sunlight, Dunne turned.

'Good day to you, McAdam. You weren't in your office so I figured I'd find you working.' He eyed the sling that Neil wore but said nothing.

'I've been apprised of your trouble. I hope your two men will be back on the job soon. Heard they were roughed up. That's something folks at Apache Bend won't tolerate.'

'We've been tolerating fights quite awhile, Mr Dunne. Reckon fighting ain't going out of fashion.'

'Now, it's you. Heard someone shot you. Goddam outrage. It must be tough working one-armed. I figured you could use some help.'

Help? Neil regarded the wealthy owner of the

Gila mine with suspicion. Caleb Dunne wasn't known for generosity or kindness.

'Thank you, Mr Dunne, but we'll manage.'

'I would not be offended if you called me Caleb.'

Neil shrugged and turned to leave. Then he stopped and faced the Gila owner again. 'By the way, has there been any word on your nephew?'

'No!' Dunne thundered. 'That foul murderer. I'll see Joel hang for killing his father. I heard there was a bounty hunter up Colorado way showing pictures and asking questions. I may just have to get one to go after Joel, Rengert's useless.'

Neil's pulses quickened. 'Bounty hunter? Who's he looking for?'

'Don't know. Good day, McAdam.' He mounted the stallion. He applied a whip to the animal's flanks as he spurred it on.

The mention of a bounty hunter bothered Neil. Was there really one as close as Colorado, showing pictures, asking questions? Or was Caleb Dunne fishing? He shook the thought.

That evening, feeling as if he were caught in a sagebrush fire, Neil tried to get comfortable on his cot. He was not successful. His left arm and shoulder throbbed. His lips and mouth were dry.

Merle Benson arrived with a light supper that she had prepared for him.

'Neil, I learned this afternoon that Mr Dunne offered us his help. Were you going to tell me?'

'I saw no reason. He came to you?'

'Yes. He brought with him his own foreman and another miner. He said they could stay with our mine a few days. So I thanked him.'

'I know Dieter Koesler. I don't trust him or Caleb

Dunne.'

'Neil, why are you so stubborn?'

She felt his forehead, his cheeks. 'Neil, you're feverish.' She put cold cloths on his forehead and face. He felt as if he had stumbled from the desert into an oasis water hole. He soon drifted off into a troubled sleep.

He was back in Georgia in '65, with his twin brother Phil, when they were both in the Confederate Army during the War Between the States. He saw the land, devastated, as General Sherman marched to the sea. He and his brother saw their father killed by one of Sherman's Yankees. They watched their heartbroken mother die. The McAdams were ruined, their homes, their crops, all destroyed.

In his dream he heard Phil vow to kill General Sherman somehow, sometime. He saw Phil raise his gun, take aim.

'No, no, no!' Neil shouted waking. He threw aside the cool cloths in Miss Benson's hands. He stared, wild-eyed, around the office. 'No, goddamit, no!' he yelled.

'Neil, what is it? You were having a nightmare.'

'I was? I don't know.' He sank back on the cot.

He really did know. The dream, the nightmare, had been with him for eight long years.

FOUR

Each day for the next two days, Merle Benson rode to the mine office to tend Neil's wound and to go over the books. She gave Koesler orders but would not let him into the office. Neil watched her with admiration. Tom Benson's daughter was some woman.

When she arrived each morning on Firefly she brought breakfast. His appetite returned and he saw that she was pleased.

'My ma always said starve a fever,' he said.

'Nonsense. You need to keep up your strength.'

She changed his dressing twice a day. At noon she brought dinner and at night she returned with supper. His heart pounded at the sight of her. Careful, she was his boss. *Miss* Benson.

His wound was healing but he knew he'd bear a scar. On Wednesday morning, his fever broke.

That afternoon he crossed with steady steps and clear head to the mine. He entered the tunnel. He found Koesler at the main shaft.

'Koesler, you and your helper can go now. Tell your boss at the Gila that we thank him.'

Dieter Koesler shifted his stocky frame to confront Neil. He seemed redder of face than usual. Neil smelled whiskey on the German's breath. It took Koesler a moment to comprehend Neil's dismissal.

'Mr Dunne tell me and Frank stay here,' the on-loan foreman said. His German accent was thick as ore dust. 'He say work until he tell me leave.'

'Caleb Dunne has no say over this mine, Koesler. I do. Now, you get your things and leave. Miss Benson will pay Dunne for your services.'

Neil put on another hat, that of foreman in place of Zack Meadows. He figured work would pick up at the Benson digs, even though Ken Vanderman could not be on hand. He hoped it wouldn't be too long before Zack and Ken were fit again.

It felt good to be hard at work after three days of idleness. Funny what a heavy slug in the arm can do to keep a man off his feet. The only thing that hampered him now was the sling Merle had made for him on her new Singer sewing machine that came by Wells Fargo.

Neil felt he had a growing stake in Apache Bend now that he had a chance to square his life. Perhaps his drifter days, the days of running, were over and he had at last found a home. It had been a long time since he had known real happiness.

He was more than pleased, too, with his 35 percent share in the Benson mine. He would never forget how Tom Benson had trusted him, gave him a permanent job. Now Merle Benson had gone her father one better. Manager was a fine big title for a man of 26.

From the day Neil started work at the Benson digs he was attracted to Merle Benson. Yet, he knew his place and he kept it. He felt comfortable at Merle's house, maybe too comfortable. She had nursed him, saw his arm heal, had worried about him.

He was worried about her as well and he knew his concern went beyond the mine. A young lady in wild country needed a man's protection. Tough as it was, he shook off for the moment his growing feelings for Merle Benson.

Without Zack Meadows and Ken Vanderman, Neil worked doubly hard at the mine the balance of the week, acting as a foreman in the tunnels and as a manager on the surface.

On Monday morning, Neil rode Dixie into Apache Bend to arrange for his day-of-the-week at the stamping mill. He shared the mill with the five other mine operators in the area. By right of size and output, Caleb Dunne's Gila Mine had first choice of days. Dunne always picked Monday, which meant his silver was shipped out ahead of the others.

The mill, centrally located for all six mines above the Apache Bend lode, broke up the ore rock so it could be chemically treated to get the silver. It was a noisy, ground-shaking process and Dixie shied away from it.

Neil found the other five mine owners at the stamping mill as they scheduled their turns. Caleb Dunne nodded but didn't speak to the others. Neil knew that some of the owners were in awe of Dunne, his wealth and his mine. His was the only one to have a name, Gila. The others were content to simply lend their own names to their mines.

Harry Hawthorne, dark-eyed and raw-boned, was back in full production after the dynamite blast at his digs. Matt Felkins kept fingering his wispy moustache as he eyed Dunne. Hawthorne and Felkins were close friends. A dozen years earlier they had been army scouts together.

Neil thanked Brad Connors again for coming along when he did the night he was shot.

'Glad I was there,' the crippled, graying, mine owner said.

Lars Olsen had the smallest operation. The pale-eyed Swede struck Neil as being cowed rather than awed by Caleb Dunne. Olsen was the only mine owner present at the stamping mill office who didn't carry a gun. Neil, as did Felkins, Hawthorne and Connors, had .44 revolvers holstered and strapped at their hips.

Dunne, Like Olsen, did not carry a sidearm. Neil saw at the saddle of Dunne's chestnut stallion, a .52 caliber Spencer repeating rifle. Was it the one that had been fired at him? He dismissed the thought. Caleb Dunne was not a killer. Another thought came and lingered. Dunne would hire a gunslinger to do the job.

After everyone was scheduled for the week, Caleb Dunne mounted his stallion and then bade the others a curt farewell.

Neil and the four remaining mine owners lingered a while to exchange pleasantries. Hawthorne inquired about Miss Benson.

'She's fine. Worried though, like the rest of us.'

Lars Olsen nodded. 'I'm right scared. I don't hanker for no explosion in my mine, I don't want my men beat up like McAdam. I don't want to be shot. Will the sheriff help us?'

'Guy Rengert ain't worth two cowpies on a silver platter,' Hawthorne spat. 'Shit, other side of that tin star is a yellow streak wide as the big canyon. Twice as wide.'

'Hell, maybe we oughtta do something ourselves,' Neil said.

'Like what?'

'Don't know. Let's ponder on it.' A plan had been forming in his mind, but he'd hold his tongue until the idea took shape.

After commenting on the weather and the silver market and the news that Ingrid Olsen was in the family way, the five men parted.

Neil rode to the general store and shopped and exchanged news. It was nearly twilight when he left, his saddle bags filled with some tinned foods, ammunition, a new razor and shaving brush, and some needles and thread that Miss Benson had asked for.

He untied and mounted Dixie without effort for he had dispensed with his sling. As he was about to spur Dixie on, he spied Amy Gentian coming toward the general store. He eyed the way she walked, the way she held her head. A pretty filly for sure.

He had seen her many times because she was Miss Benson's friend, but he had never spoken to Apache Bend's school ma'am. Half the young bucks in town, too old for school, had done so. They hung around the little schoolhouse beyond the church hoping to get a glimpse of her when she left for Millie Hawthorne's where she roomed and boarded. Neil had not been near this schoolhouse or any classroom for ten years.

She raised her hand to halt Neil before he rode off.

'Neil McAdam, you're as shy as a boy, first day at school. Cat got your tongue?'

'No, ma'am, Miss Gentian.'

'My the man talks!'

Neil smiled. 'A man ought to have something to

say before he opens his mouth. That's a mighty pretty bonnet. What's on your mind, Miss Gentian?'

'The box social 4th of July night. It's going to be at the school yard.'

'Hadn't heard about it, ma'am.'

'Course not. Some of the ladies just decided. Millie Hawthorne, Betsy Vanderman and Dolly Meadows are organizing it.'

'Box socials are fun. We had them back home, too. Fellows got to eat supper with their girls.'

'There'll be square dancing. Doc Whitman's calling.'

'What they going to do with the money?'

'Now if that isn't like a man!' She smiled. 'Half of it goes to help pay my keep and the other half goes to help pay the parson's. You'll bring Merle Benson, won't you?'

Startled at the thought he almost spurred Dixie. 'Well, I don't reckon I know.'

He tipped his hat, said good-evening, and rode away.

Bring Miss Benson? Not likely, but it sure would be fun.

Half way back to the mine he muttered. 'Well, why not?'

Two thirds there he spoke again. 'Think I should, Dixie?'

He reached the office, then tethered and groomed his mustang in the lean-to. 'I'll ask her to mark her box somehow,' he said half-aloud. 'Blue ribbon or something, so's I'll know it and be high bidder for it.'

Coming to the front of the office he saw the shift was buttoning up the mine for the day. Dusk had settled and shadows were deepening into the mine's surroundings, then disappearing. He was about to enter the office when one of his crewmen shouted.

'Neil! Watch out! Move your ass!'

Neil spun round and glanced up. A heavy wagon, loaded with ore rock, which had been parked on a small rise nearby, now rolled toward the office and himself. It picked up speed quickly and continued on a straight course of destruction.

Neil leaped to safety.

The wagon slammed into the office, crashing half-way through it, sending pieces of adobe brick and wood beams flying in every direction.

FIVE

Neil caught a glimpse of a shadow-like figure running away from the hilltop. The man vanished in the darkness.

Peering inside the wreckage of his office, Neil saw that the ore-laden wagon rested atop his flattened cot. Had he stepped inside a moment sooner, to sit at the small desk or lie on his cot, he would have been crushed.

'What a Monday,' he muttered as he wiped ore dust from his eyes, 'there's somebody who doesn't like me very much, I swear.'

Ned Lockhart and two other men of Neil's crew ran toward him. The first to reach him spoke.

'You okay, boss?'

'Jim, I figure you warned me just in time. Thanks.'

'Shit, least I could do, boss.'

'Somebody gave that goddam wagon a shove,' Ned Lockhart said. His voice expressed both concern and rage. 'Only a two-legged sonovabitch would do that.'

'Reckon you're right, Ned. I saw someone up there take off like a jackrabbit. Too dark to make him out.' Neil shook his head. 'Cinch it couldn't start up by itself. And sure as hell won't move outta

the office by itself either. Jim, Pete, get your horses
and some ropes from the digs. We'll need 'em for
sure.'

Ten minutes later the two crewmen were back
with their horses. They tied the ends of the ropes
to the wagon and to the saddle horns. Ned, Jim and
Pete put their shoulders to the wagon and they
urged the horses on. Neil had removed the sling
from his left arm that day and he added his
strength to the others.

Within a few minutes the four men and two
horses had managed to remove the wagon from
the office and settle it a few yards beyond.

'We'll stick around and help clean up the place,'
Jim offered.

Ned shook his head. 'No, I'll stay with McAdam.
You two finish buttoning up the digs. Look sharp
while you're at it.'

'Thanks, men,' Neil said, as Jim and Pete
departed.

Neil and Ned shook their heads at the wrecked
Benson office. Two of the adobe walls that formed
a corner opposite from where the wagon had
smashed through were still intact. The roof at
those two standing walls was solid, but then it
sagged and sloped toward the floor and the two
sides of the structure that had been crushed.

The desk had changed into kindling and the
mine's files lay among the shattered drawers. Neil's
cot was as flat as an Arizona mesa. The plank table
and the Franklin stove survived the wagon's
onslaught.

Ned grasped a fallen beam and he and Neil
propped up one corner of the sagging roof. They
did the same at another corner. Neil lit several

lanterns and set them on the plank table.

'Looks like your bed ain't worth much, Neil. You can bunk in at my place if you've a mind to. The wife's visiting her sister over at Bentling's Corner.'

'Thanks, Ned. First, I better get these files over to Miss Benson's , then I'll stop in at your place if the invitation still holds.'

After Ned had checked the mine button-up and rode off, Neil packed two saddle bags with the mine's records and the purchases he had made for himself and Merle Benson.

He saddled the nervous Dixie again and then headed for the mine owner's house. It was late now and he wasn't sure if his boss would be up. A light in her kitchen window told him that she was still awake. He hitched Dixie to the porch rail and then knocked at the kitchen door.

She opened it. He saw her look of surprise, then a growing smile that erased surprise from her face. She gave a small cry of delight.

'Neil, for heaven's sake!' The smile on her face was as bright as the smile in her voice.

'I brought you the needles and thread you wanted, Miss Benson, and supplies, tinned foods, lantern wicks, that I got for myself.'

'Needles and thread?' She laughed. 'At this time of night?'

'I fetched more 'n that. I've got the mine's records here. Best you keep them for a spell.'

He carried the saddle bags in and set them on her kitchen table. He sniffed and grinned.

'You're baking a cake. Smelled it a mile away.'

'Never mind what I'm baking. What happened, Neil?'

He told her of the ore wagon and the demolition of half the office. His voice was grave, supporting the worry-frown across his brow. His deep blue eyes narrowed. 'We've got a fox in the henhouse.'

Her face had paled as she listened to his account. 'My God, Neil, you could have been killed!'

'Sure, that's the truth.'

'You can't sleep there any longer.'

'Won't have to for a bit. Ned Lockhart says he'll put me up for a few days while the crew gets everything back in shape. Then I'll put in my nights back there again. I reckon someone's after your digs. They went after your father, they've gone after me. They'll keep at it, trying to scare you I think. Maybe someone's after more than your digs. Maybe someone wants the whole damned lode. Hey, you gonna offer me a piece of that cake?'

She sighed. 'It's not frosted, but if you'll wait, yes.'

'All right.' He hesitated for a moment then straightened his shoulders. 'Miss Benson, I met Miss Amy Gentian at the general store this afternoon. She tells me there's gonna be a box social come Friday, 4th of July.'

'I know.'

'I was wondering, would it be okay, would I be asking too much, I mean would you pleasure me by allowing me to take you there?'

She just stood there, letting him stammer on.

'If you'll go with me, maybe you'd put a big bright ribbon on your box supper so's I could outbid any fellow who'd be after it.' He gave a great, relieved sigh. 'Miss Gentian said I should ask.'

The moment he admitted that, he knew he had put his foot in his mouth, complete with sock and boot and spur.

'Neil McAdam! You get yourself shot, two of your best men are attacked and hurt in the Sagebrush Saloon, my office is wrecked, and you asked me if I'd go to a piddling little box social. What's worse, you tell me Amy Gentian put you up to it. You're impossible!'

'Yes, Miss Benson. Well, will you give me the pleasure?'

Her eyes sparkled in the kitchen's lantern light. 'Of course I'll go with you, Neil. You should have known that before you asked.'

On Tuesday, the day after the near destruction of the office, a crew hand-picked by Ned Lockhart set to work repairing the interior damage and rebuilding the two walls that were flattened. The adobe bricks were fitted snugly and set with strong mortar.

One of the crew, a half-white, half-Navajo whom Tom Benson had hired before Neil's day, offered a suggestion more tuned to Neil's six-foot frame.

'I can make you a bed, twice as comfortable to sleep on than the one you had. Indian style bed.'

'I'd appreciate that, Thunder Cloud.'

On that same Tuesday, a complacent Caleb Dunne sat in his own office, the headquarters of the Gila silver mine to the north of Apache Bend. The Gila operation was the largest, most profitable one in the string of six mines stretching across the mother lode.

Caleb Dunne leaned back in his chair and

surveyed the office from wall to wall. Then he glanced out the window to the broad entrance of the Gila tunnel. His black eyes gleamed with satisfaction at the sight.

'All mine,' he gloated. He smiled at his spoken thought.

The Gila operation was, in truth, his alone, and had been ever since the murder three months earlier of his brother Howard. Howard Dunne had been co-owner. Caleb's bothersome nephew, Howard's motherless son, was heir to his father's half-ownership. Joel Dunne, however, was unlikely to show up to claim his share, or to show himself around Apache Bend. The boy's face was on posters all over the county.

Caleb Dunne had insisted in the presence of Sheriff Guy Rengert that 18-year old Joel Dunne had murdered his own father. Caleb, in a sworn statement, attested that he had witnessed the shooting. Before the young killer could be arrested, he disappeared into the Arizona hills. Joel Dunne must be found. Nephew or not, the kid must hang. Only then would Caleb feel secure in the full ownership of the Gila. He rose from his chair and crossed to a large map on his office wall. It was roughly drawn but the scale was accurate.

He traced a line drawn in a curve from north to south. At the northern end of the line was his own digs, the Gila. At the southern end was Miss Benson's mine. At the center of the line, but slightly to the west, was Apache Bend. The town did not rest astride the argentite lode.

South of the Gila was Harry Hawthorne's digs, now back in operation after the explosion. Rotten luck! Dunne was sure Hawthorne would be finished, but there he was back in production. South of Hawthorne's mine was Lars Olsen's. Well, that snivelling damned Swede couldn't last much longer, especially since Olsen's wife seemed eager to leave Apache Bend.

South of Apache Bend, along the curved line, was Brad Connors' operation. That cripple would soon be limping out of town. Yet Connors was stubborn, and so was his foreman Grant Tennant.

South of Connors was Matt Felkins' digs. Tough as his army scout sidekick of a dozen years ago, Harry Hawthorne, Matt Felkins posed a problem. Caleb knew it was Felkins who pitched in quickly to help put Hawthorne back on his feet.

Then, finally, at the curved line's southernmost tip, there was the Benson mine. Too bad the cave-in and Tom Benson's death didn't daunt pretty Miss Merle Benson any more than a coyote's howl at a full moon. He hadn't counted on Merle Benson sticking it out.

He blamed Neil McAdam for Tom Benson's daughter's decision to hang on to her father's mine. Without that young southerner around to run things, she'd probably have left town right after her father's death.

He stared at the pins stuck in at each of the mines' locations, including his own. Keep the pasteboards close to his vest, don't try to fill an inside straight, don't try to draw to a flush. He'd not gamble on making the other mines part of the Gila just yet.

He left his office and crossed to the tunnel entrance of the Gila. Dieter Koesler, his foreman, was usually there, watching the ore cars as they emerged from the tunnel.

He spotted Koesler and called him aside.

'I want you to make sure that next week a little accident happens to a mine. I want it to occur on Friday, 4th of July.'

'Sure, Mr Dunne,' came the strong guttural accents of Koesler. 'Whose?'

'Ours, goddamit!'

The stolid German showed no surprise.

'Where will you be, boss?'

'At the box social in the schoolyard in Apache Bend.'

Dunne turned and headed back to his office. Maybe the key to the Benson mine was charm, a liberal helping with a little gallantry thrown in for good measure. Women tumbled for that every time. He'd be sure to make the highest bid on Miss Merle's pretty box supper. Who knows, maybe she'd also give him a sample of what was under her gingham.

SIX

By mid-afternoon Saturday just two days before the end of June, and exactly as Ned Lockhart had promised, the crew, including Thunder Cloud, had readied Neil's office for use once more. In one of the new, strong adobe walls, a broad window had been added. It provided a clear view of the tunnel entrance to the Benson mine. Neil could ascertain at a glance what activity was taking place on the surface of the digs, who was entering the mine and who was coming out.

His new, longer and wider plank desk now boasted three drawers on either side of the kneehole. Ample room, too, to hold the mine's records and ledgers, and that satisfied Neil immensely.

Thunder Cloud had contributed his native skills to assure that the office was also ready to sleep in again. Neil watched with keen interest as the halfbreed assembled the Indian-style bed that he had promised.

'Boss, this is a bed that you will not want to leave when the sun rises.'

Thunder Cloud had brought with him a number of slim branches of the bushy paloverde tree. There had been no need to trim the small leaves. The limbs were leafless most of the year. Neil had seen the green-bark trees growing as high as 20 feet or more in the barren, arid regions south of Apache Bend. The branches were tough yet pliable. Thunder Cloud, with deft fingers, interwove short lengths in and out across longer lengths to create a sturdy web. This he laced with rawhide on to two thicker branches.

Next, Thunder Cloud made three frames of paloverde branches and rawhide strips, each frame four feet wide by two feet in height, each well cross-braced. He placed the travois platform atop the three frames and secured it well with thongs of the cured hide. Finally, he placed atop the webbed platform-bed three buffalo robes, their shaggy yet curly gray hair upwards. They offered a mattress that invited no comparison.

Thunder Cloud stood up from his labors and smiled. 'You lie down, boss, you will see that you won't want to get up.'

Somewhat embarrassed in front of the crew, Neil stretched out on his new bed. There was room to spare for his six-foot frame.

'I swear, Thunder Cloud, this is something.'

The half-breed grinned. 'There is room enough for two, boss.'

'Shut up, Thunder Cloud!' Ned Lockhart said.

The men left and Neil, as Thunder Cloud had prophecied, was reluctant to stir from his bed of buffalo robes.

As Neil relaxed in the restored office, a slim man, with a map of dogged determination spread across his features rode through the lonely, northeast desert country of Arizona territory.

He asked anyone he came across a never-varying question:

'Have you seen this man? Here's his picture. Name of Neil McAdam. Have you seen him?'

The man received few answers to his questions. The answers he did get were always *no*. In the territories, most men, whether miners or prospectors, cattlemen or sodbusters, had little affection for bounty hunters. The slim rider knew that. He moved on, riding south, always asking 'Have you seen this man?'

On Friday, the 4th of July, just as the sun was vanishing beyond the hills, Neil rode Dixie to the Benson house. Merle was waiting for him on the front porch. His eyes widened at the sight of her. Was there ever a girl who was prettier? She had brightened her soft brown curls with a yellow ribbon. She wore a dress as blue as a summer sky, with puffed sleeves and a low neckline. Around her waist she wore another yellow ribbon as a sash.

She held an oblong box wrapped in a blue cloth and tied, as were her curls and her dress, with a yellow ribbon.

He let loose with a rebel yell as he dismounted and gazed at the picture of feminine loveliness before him.

'Neil McAdam, what on earth on you staring at?'

'Miss Benson,' he grinned, 'with all that blue and yellow I thought you were the prettiest cavalry officer I reckon I've seen. If you were such an officer I swear I'd join up.' He glanced again at her blue and yellow dress. 'You gonna ride back of me on Dixie?'

'No, Neil McAdam, I'm not. We'll go in style. You can tether Dixie in the shed and hitch up dad's bay to the buckboard.'

'Which bay? Alden or Standish?'

Her brown eyes sparkled. 'Why don't you choose for yourself, Neil?'

He walked Dixie to the shed behind the house and tethered the mustang to an iron ring in the stall. He debated a moment and then selected Alden for the drive into Apache Bend.

He drove around to the front of the house where Merle Benson waited. He was about to help her up but she was beside him before he realized it. One thing for sure, Miss Benson could do whatever she had a mind to.

'I guess I'll know for sure which is your box supper, what with the yellow ribbon and all. What's inside to eat?'

'I'm not telling, Neil.'

'I reckon I'll just have to bid the sky to find out. I'll do it!'

His eyes shone as they approached the school-yard on the south side of Apache Bend. The lights came into view first, then the sound of Homer Breithalter's fiddle and the stomping of booted feet.

There came a halt to the square dance and the music as Neil and Merle drove up. Neil noticed some winks from the married men and nudges by their ladies as the two drew the buckboard alongside other wagons. Neil tethered Alden to the hitching rail alongside the little adobe school. Merle took her box supper to the long table set under some alamo trees nearby, while Neil looked around with almost boyish pleasure. A decade had passed since he had been to a box social as a lad of sixteen. Memories of soldiers and girls in crinoline hoopskirts who danced cotillions and flirted under the great oak trees at his home. The men bid excessive amounts for a young lady's box supper. Most always the soldiers in gray won out. Then the lucky bidder and the girl would drift off among the trees to share the supper while the young male slaves would poke each other and snicker as they watched.

He wrenched himself back to the present. The past was lost forever to Neil McAdam.

Millie Hawthorne, Betsy Vanderman and Dolly Meadows had ringed the schoolyard with lanterns hung high on poles. In the center, Harry Hawthorne, with the help of Eddie Cox, had built a wooden platform for dancing. Ken Vanderman and Zack Meadows, still somewhat incapacitated from the beatings they suffered in Eddie's saloon, could do little more than sit on the sidelines and toss good-natured jibes at Hawthorne. Zack Meadows called out: 'Looks like you tore up half the damn sidewalk in front of the Sagebrush, Harry, so's you could rig up that platform for a little dos-a-dos.'

'Talk's cheap, men, when you know I can't light into a man with a clipped wing and one with a hobble on his leg.'

Ken laughed. 'Ain't dance space enough, Harry, for a bit of *Coming Through the Rye*.'

Neil was always astonished every time he heard Breithalter play. The smithy, whose huge, powerful hands could shoe any man's horse, stallion or mare, with the utmost ease, could also coax beautiful, haunting music from his violin. He would favor Apache Bend with Mozart and Haydn. He would give them, if they wished, lively strains for a square dance, a Virginia reel or a Texas two-step. Sometimes, with a little arm-twisting by Parson Gabriel Ashe, Homer could be induced to play a hymn or two in church.

Gabriel Ashe had been an itinerant circuit rider of unknown religious persuasion who rode into Apache Bend two years earlier. The town lacked a preacher ever since Parson Uranus Isley wandered too far into the mountains and tumbled to his death in a thirty-foot crevice.

Sheriff Guy Rengert and Doc Whitman offered Ashe the position of preacher at five dollars a week. When he told them that his name, Gabriel, meant Man of God, they promptly doubled his salary. The town had a devil of a time meeting it, as it also had to come up with the wages for the school teacher, Amy Gentian.

Homer Breithalter returned to the dance floor edge and sat on a keg that had once held sorghum. Doc Whitman, as caller for the square dance, stood on the opposite side of the fiddler. Everyone in Apache Bend acknowledged that no man could call the steps as well as he could.

Doc Whitman held up his hand and shouted for everyone's attention. He took off his hat and his white hair shone under the lanterns.

'Folks, we all know why we're here tonight. We don't want Miss Gentian and Parson Ashe to go looking for greener pastures. Now, I'm going to set my hat down and you folks feel free to drop a dollar in it to go along with the auction. All right then, gentlemen, choose your ladies.'

After a moment the strains of *Old Dan Hummer* echoed across the schoolyard.

Doc Whitman's calls came fast and lively.

'First couples bow to your partners …
'Second couples you do the same …
'First couples bow to your corners …
'Second couples put 'em to shame!'

And so it went for the next half hour. Call after call. Most of the couples knew the steps. When they didn't and collided into the others they would laugh and try to get back into the swing. Neil knew only a few of the moves, but Merle was familiar with all of them. She managed to guide her manager through them without him tripping over his two left feet.

In a grand-right-and-left he came face to face with Amy Gentian twice and each time she whispered to him during the brief moment their hands clasped.

'Now aren't you glad, Neil McAdam, that you brought Merle Benson?'

He had no time to answer.

'What did Amy Gentian say to you?' Merle asked him when they joined in a grand promenade.

Neil smiled and white-lied. 'She told me she thought it was time you went out with me, Miss Benson.'

Fifteen minutes later, just as Doc Whitman prepared to call for bids on the box suppers, Caleb Dunne rode up on his chestnut stallion, tethered it and strode toward the dance floor. He turned to Merle Benson. 'I do want to offer my sympathies about the damage to your office, ma'am. If there's anything I can do, just let me know.'

Before Merle Benson had a chance to reply, Doc Whitman started the bidding. Box after attractively-wrapped box brought top dollars.

Some husbands managed to eat with their wives; some young bachelors found, to their dismay, they'd be dining with matrons. Stuttering Grant Tennant, foreman at the Connors Mine, claimed Amy Gentian's polka-dotted package. A few moments after that, Doc Whitman picked up the blue box with the yellow ribbon.

Neil knew to whom it belonged. He saw Caleb Dunne glance at Merle Benson's blue dress with the yellow sash, then eye the box in Doc Whitman's hand, then return his thoughtful look to Merle. Neil understood at once that Caleb Dunne had made the connection.

'One dollar for the blue box!' Dunne called out.

'Two dollars,' Neil countered.

The bidding went as high as six dollars.

Neil groaned inwardly. Six dollars was a lot of money, yet he was determined Caleb Dunne would not sup with Merle Benson tonight.

'Seven dollars!' Neil shouted.

'Seven dollars!' Doc Whitman echoed. 'Do I hear seven-fifty?'

Caleb Dunne held up his hand to interrupt, but before he could raise the bid, Dieter Koesler galloped up on a palomino, dismounted, and yelled to his boss.

'Mr Dunne! Mr Dunne!'

'What is it, Koesler?'

'The mine! The Gila!' His thick German accent grew more pronounced as he spoke. 'There's been a cave-in. There's a fire there now. Much damage, I think! Better you come now!'

Dunne leaped on his horse. Some miners made ready to join him, to see what could be done to help out at the Gila. Dunne faced Neil.

'Damn you, McAdam! You've won this time.' His voice was edged with a note of warning. 'You may not be so lucky next time, remember that! Enjoy the fireworks! Enjoy your supper!'

SEVEN

The news of another mine cave-in, this time at the Gila, had a sobering effect at the Apache Bend box social. Neil enjoyed the ham and chicken sandwiches and chocolate cake that Merle Benson had prepared, but the angry departure of Caleb Dunne ruined what had been a gala affair. For a while, most of the Independence Day revellers ate in silence once the attractively-wrapped boxes had been opened.

Neil and Merle sat at one of the tables a few feet from the makeshift dance floor. A nearby lantern lent a soft glow to their features. As they ate and drank the cool lemonade, they listened to a stirring oration by Parson Gabriel Ashe.

'Our country's shy a couple of years from being a century old,' Ashe intoned. 'Arizona Territory here, was settled at the same time our nation was born. It's not even a state yet but its day will come, fear not.' He made a sweeping gesture with his arm that Neil felt took in all of Arizona Territory and territories beyond.

Now, after Parson Ashe's speech, Neil, like a boy of lesser years, was awed by the brilliant display of fireworks. Weeks earlier, Frank Yegelstrom had ordered skyrockets, Roman Candles and Pinwheels from St. Louis. Tonight, many of them lit up the flag with its 13 stripes and 37 stars. Would Arizona some day put another star on the union?

Square dancing, box supper, oratory and fireworks could not blot out the feeling of guilt Neil harbored for not riding off with a few of the other men to see how they might lend a hand at the Gila.

'A man oughtta see what he can do,' he insisted to Merle.

'Well, I didn't see any of the other owners rush to help out.'

'No ma'am. It sure seems like Caleb Dunne hasn't got many friends. Still, a man oughtta see what he can do.'

'Oh, you're just like my daddy!' She pouted prettily. 'He was always talking about being a man and not half a man, and the silly ways men measure other men.'

Neil rose. 'Yes ma'am. I reckon being just like Tom Benson would be something to be mighty proud of.'

'Thank you, Neil.'

'That was a mighty tasty supper. I reckon just about everyone here, except Caleb Dunne, had a right good time. Now, Miss Benson, it'll be time to drive you home.'

The day after Independence Day, Neil rode to Yegelstrom's General Store to pack his saddlebags with supplies for Merle and himself. Rather than taking the buckboard, he preferred to ride Dixie.

He tethered his mustang to the hitching post and then ambled in to the store. He sniffed. He always liked the rich odor of spices and dry goods that filled the air inside. The spices were a lure to the womenfolk, as were the bolts of calico and gingham. Mingled with the aroma was the smell of leather that came from boots, saddles and sets of harness.

The only jarring note this Saturday afternoon was the presence of the stolid Dieter Koesler. The German foreman at the Gila was trying to get Yegelstrom to lower his price on a horsewhip.

'Can't,' said the store owner. 'Them's genuine cowhide lashes strung at the end of the whip. Handle's tooled cowhide, too. Bought the lot of them whips from a drummer passing through from 'Frisco.'

'It is for Mr Dunne.'

'I don't care if it's for Brig Young or any of his hundred wives. Price is what it says there. If Caleb Dunne doesn't like it tell him to cut an alamo switch.'

'I am not wanting that whip I don't think.' Koesler turned aside.

'Hold on a minute,' Neil said.

'What you want?'

'Some details about the cave-in at the Gila yesterday. You said there was damage. Anyone hurt?'

'No. It was the holiday 4th of July. No one working.'

Neil's blue eyes hardened. 'What happened, Koesler?'

Koesler shifted uneasily and turned to leave. 'I must get back to the Gila.'

Yegelstrom added his own request. 'Maybe you should answer McAdam's questions. I'd like to know what happened, too. I got a small investment in Dunne's mine.' He turned to Neil. 'Didn't make it with Caleb Dunne. I put a couple of hundred dollars in his brother's hands. Howard was a good man. Figure Caleb's using my money now since he's taken over the Gila and Howie's son, Joel, is gone and missing like he'd been hung.' He turned back to Koesler. 'Talk, dammit!'

'Everything quiet at the mine all day. Mr Dunne he ride away to town. I enjoy a schnapps from the old country for the holiday when I heard rumble. I go to the mine and walk in the tunnel. I look down the first shaft. It is filled with timber and rocks at the next level. The walls of the shaft caved in. No way to get down. I know no one is below. I ride to get Mr Dunne.'

Koelser's hesitant account seemed straightforward enough, but Neil's thoughts raced back to several months earlier. Tons of earth that gave way. Shattered timbers reduced to matchsticks. The rocks. And beneath them the crushed body of Tom Benson. The sudden recall caused a chill, like the touch of an icy hand, that raised the blond hairs at the back of his neck.

The Gila cave-in was exactly like that in the Benson Mine.

Coincidence? Probably. Cave-ins are cave-ins. No one was in the Gila mine because of the celebration, but Tom Benson was in his digs – the wrong place at the wrong time. Had someone known Benson would be there? Odd.

Neil nodded curtly as the German left.

After purchasing his supplies, Neil rode the few miles north to the Gila's office. Koesler was nowhere in sight. Neil could not tell if Dunne's foreman had returned to give an account of the confrontation with Yegelstrom at the general store.

Neil found Dunne at his desk in the well-appointed office.

'Afternoon, McAdam. What brings you here?' He looked beyond Neil where he could see, through the office window, the Benson's manager's mount. 'Of course, your horse.' He smiled, but the smile was not friendly. 'A fine looking mustang you got there, McAdam.'

'There's no horse like Dixie. That horse is sure part of me.'

'Like I said, what brings you here?'

'I'm sorry that you had an accident at the mine. I hope the damage wasn't too bad.' Neil eyed Dunne carefully. Did Dunne know that Koesler had already described the cave-in? Dunne gave no sign.

'Nothing that can't be repaired in time. We'll weather it.'

'Now, Dunne, you're under attack like the rest of us.'

'You didn't come here to offer your sympathy, McAdam.'

'I reckon you have that right. Before anything else happens that nobody wants to happen, I think all of us should form some kind of Miners' Protective Association. You being the most influential of us ought to head it up.'

Neil was startled at the way the idea that had been simmering in his mind came so quickly into focus.

Dunne leaned back, slapped his thigh, and laughed.

'McAdam, that's the stupidest idea I've ever heard. I'll overlook it because it didn't come from a mine owner.' The laugh lines reformed into the frown creases that usually resided on his face. 'It won't work, McAdam. Goddamit, it never will!'

'Why not?'

'I'll tell you why not. It'll only cause more harassment. Whoever's behind all this will resent a show of strength. Defiance, and that's what you're suggesting, only invites anger and vengeance. Now, if you'll excuse me, I've work to do. Haven't you?'

Neil departed. When he arrived an hour later at Merle's house he told her of his idea.

'I'd like to invite the mine owners, their foremen, wives of those who have a wife, and lay out my idea. Could we have the meeting in your parlor, Miss Benson? It's short notice, but I'd like to invite them over tomorrow afternoon, after church.'

'Why not? I'll make refreshments.'

'We should let them know tonight.' He hesitated. 'I don't know if they'll listen to me, not being an owner and all.'

Her brown eyes twinkled. 'Want me to come along?'

'I'd be obliged.'

They left the house. Neil waited while Merle saddled Firefly. A few minutes later, they rode alongside each other as they headed north. It was late afternoon. They knew they had many stops to make. They had no idea when they would be finished with Neil's mission.

They stopped first at Matt Felkins' home, then moved on to Brad Connors. Next it was Lars Olsen's home, where Neil and Merle were invited to have supper. Finally they met with Harry Hawthorne.

At each of the mine owners' houses, after brief

exchanges of pleasantries about the square dance and box social, Neil outlined his plan and Merle extended the invitation to meet at her place. Each invitation was enthusiastically accepted.

It was quite dark when, as they returned, they stopped briefly at the Benson mine office. The full moon was almost half-eaten away but it shed light on the ore wagon that had been pulled away from the wrecked office.

'Hold on a second, Miss Benson. I want to take a look at that wagon.'

He dismounted and then crawled under the wagon. He struck a match and examined a wheel. He did the same with the three other wheels. He felt along the axles. Nothing seemed to have been tampered with. How could it have rolled so easily into the adobe office? Probably because it was at the crest of a hill. Several men could have simply pushed it. They wouldn't have needed horses to help them out. Who, then, was the lone shadowy figure he had seen at the hilltop for a moment and who had quickly vanished?

He heard Merle dismount and walk Firefly away from him and toward the office.

Then he heard a scream, followed by another.

He slid out from under the wagon and raced toward Merle who stood at the entrance of the office.

She screamed again.

Propped against the office door was the wooden marker from Tom Benson's grave. Someone had scrawled a message across Benson's name and the years of his birth and death. The message read:

You want to protect the mine owners! You better protect Tom Benson's daughter!

Tom Benson's daughter had ceased screaming. She leaned on Neil's shoulder as she gave way to sobs.

EIGHT

Neil tried to comfort the sobbing Merle Benson with awkward expressions of 'there, there, Miss Benson, don't fret,' and 'please, ma'am, don't take on so.' He was unskilled at dealing with a crying female. He repeated over and over that he'd see that no harm would befall her.

At last she quieted and just stood by him, letting his arms hold her. Her curls fell over his broad shoulders. He was conscious that this was the closest intimacy they had ever shared. The nearness of her caused long pent-up feelings to well up within him, feelings that were far removed from the simple respect he had always paid her, feelings a country mile distant from that of a manager for his boss, feelings that churned his groin.

Her scent, her warmth, her touch, was intoxicating in the moonlight and he became drunk with her presence. He mustered every inner strength, all the power of his will to free her from his arms. He took his bandana and gently wiped away her tears, yet a small teardrop lingered in the corner of each brown eye.

'Oh, Neil, how could they do this to my daddy's memory?'

He held his tongue. There was no need to tell her that whoever was responsible for the desecration did not have her father's memory in mind. The threat was against her and himself, and he knew that he must be more vigilant than ever if he was to assure protection for them both. He was sure he could give full measure of himself if attacked. He was handy with his fists and quick with his .44. Miss Benson, however, was vulnerable and defenseless.

When he spoke again it was only to say 'I reckon if anyone tries to hurt you, Miss Benson, they'll answer to me.'

The time had raced past midnight before Merle and he managed to scrub her father's grave marker free from the threat scrawled on it. It took many applications of soap, hot water, a stiff-bristled brush and Neil's muscle. He had no idea what the culprit used to scrawl his warning. Tom Benson's name and the dates that marked his lifespan had been chiseled into the wood by Homer Breithalter, the smithy, and they were not destroyed.

'We'll take it back to the cemetery in the morning,' Neil promised. 'On the way to church.'

'No, no, no!' Merle was determined in her denial. 'I don't want anyone to see us return it where it belongs. I don't want anyone to know what happened. I don't want anyone to know that I've seen this.'

'I'll take it back to the cemetery tonight.'

They went outside. As before, he placed the wooden marker across the saddle on his patient mustang. He hesitated a moment on the porch as he said goodnight.

'Good morning, really,' she whispered. This time her brown eyes twinkled, but not with tears.

On an impulse so strong that he could not resist it, one so unpremeditated that it astonished him, he kissed her on her cheek. It was so gentle a kiss that his lips were but a light touch.

She didn't draw back. She clung to him. He kissed her again, this time on the lips. She returned his kiss. He could tell that her hunger for him was as great as that of his for her.

He knew that he had always desired her, knew it from the moment Tom Benson hired him. But he had always kept his place. More, he had kept his distance except for the need for contact during work and the business of the Benson mine. Earlier that evening was the second time he had touched her. The first was when they square-danced. When she had changed his dressing, her touch gave him pleasure more than she could know. It was a pleasure that alleviated pain.

Now, the pain caused by the desecration of Tom Benson's grave marker had led to their lips meeting in a kiss that stirred him from his blond hair to his spurred boots.

'Neil, oh Neil,' she murmured.

'Merle, little darling.' His heart raced like a road runner.

She broke from his embrace and suddenly gave a girlish giggle, a reaction so at odds with the sobs that had earlier wracked her petite figure.

'At last, you've called me Merle.'

'Yes, ma'am.'

'And there'll be no more Miss Benson and ma'am.'

'I reckon not. If I've overstepped my bounds, I'm sorry.'

'If you hadn't, I'd have overstepped them for

you.'

'If it's all right – if you're willing, I reckon I might come to call. I mean not a business call. I mean I can't ask your father.'

'A gentleman caller is always welcome, even in Arizona.'

'Don't reckon I'm that much of a gentleman.'

'You're a man. One of the gentlest and bravest I've ever known.'

'I hope I'm brave when I need to be.'

She bade him goodbye. Then she went back into her house, closed the door, and he heard her push a heavy chair against it.

'Not much protection,' he muttered as he mounted Dixie. 'I swear by all that's holy that no harm'll come to her.' With that vow, he headed back for Apache Bend and the little churchyard cemetery.

An hour later, he had restored Tom Benson's marker to its rightful place. He packed earth around it for support. He looked down upon the grave for a moment and whispered. 'I love your daughter, Tom. I will take care of her always. I promise.'

He paused briefly at the grave of Martha Whitman. He remembered her as a good, kind woman who put up with Doc's outrageous tales of the days he served with Sam Houston in the campaign against Santa Anna. He straightened a flower-filled vase on a stranger's resting place. He wondered if there was anyone who might see that the graves of Samuel and Flora McAdam were not neglected. Would he ever see Georgia again?

He rode away quickly from the cemetery. He was sure no one had seen him come and go.

Upon his return to his office, he took time to loosely tether and rub down Dixie in the adjoining lean-to. The mustang seemed more quiet than usual and Neil figured his beloved horse was just plumb tuckered out. Falling into his sometime habit of talking to his mount, he voiced his thoughts.

'It's been a busy Saturday, boy. You've been back and forth, north and south of Apache Bend so many times you've lost count. You deserve a good long rest. You take care of yourself tonight, you hear?'

Inside the office he undressed quickly in the dark and then sprawled on his comfortable bed of paloverde branches and buffalo robes. The palest of moonlight lingered at a corner of the room.

His thoughts turned to the morrow. Would someone give himself away at church when he noticed Tom Benson's marker was where it belonged? Would someone who could do such a cowardly deed even be at church?

Next, he went over in his mind what he might say to the mine owners in Merle's parlor on Sunday afternoon. Would they accept his proposition? He knew they would if Merle supported it. She should support it, he told himself, because it was the only way they could handle the mysterious happenings in the mines of late.

Just before he fell into troubled sleep, he thought of the rumored bounty hunter in the territory. Who was he after? Joel Dunne? Where might that scared kid be? Hiding somewhere, no doubt, in mortal fear of his Uncle Caleb Dunne.

Neil knew what it was like to be frightened. It was fright now that haunted his dreams. The

dream turned into a nightmare image of a vengeful
Caleb Dunne. Then Dunne was gone and General
Wiiliam Tecumseh Sherman had taken the mine
owner's place.

1865. Durham, Carolina. A sun-drenched April
afternoon.

There sat Sherman on his horse. Pride and
impatience were written on the general's features.
Neil stared, awe-struck at the commander of the
Army of Tennessee, the man who led troops in
battle at Bull Run, Shiloh and Vicksburg. Neil and
his twin brother, Phil, were, once more, in his
dream, in the Confederate troops being surren-
dered by General J E Johnston.

Sherman sat his horse well. It was a great, dappled
mare that pawed the ground as if in a hurry to get
the surrender ceremony over with. Johnston sat
equally tall in the saddle. His black gelding stood
steadfast but his head was bowed to the ground.

How real everything was yet all the while Neil was
aware that it was a dream. The sights, the sounds,
the smell of sweat from men and horses. The ring of
bugle calls, the piping of fifes, the roll of drums,
assailed Neil's ears and nostrils. He saw himself
caught up in the solemnity of the occasion. He was
aware that the war was coming to an end, but defeat
had left a bitter taste on his lips. He knew it was even
more bitter on the lips of Phil.

Young, tired men of his and Phil's age were lined
up in rows before Sherman. They had tried to clean
and patch their uniforms so as not to surrender
pride along with their bodies. Neil and his brother
and the Confederate soldiers in the ranks tried to
hold back their tears. They refused to be shamed.

They stared straight ahead, as they always did in

his dream, when the Union troops hauled down the Stars and Bars. Some cursed under their breath. One by one they prepared to hand over their rifles to the victors. The weapons were destined for Union wagons.

He and his twin stood side by side in the front rank of his infantry company, Phil to his right. They were so close to Sherman that they could see the sneer, the arrogance that marked his features. this was the man who had burned and pillaged his way through Georgia to the sea. This was the man who had destroyed the heritage that had once been the pride of Neil and Phil.

Neil saw himself, the younger twin by seven minutes, inclined to want the surrender ceremony over as fast as possible. He wanted to get on with his life as soon as the enemy permitted. Phil was unforgiving. Neil had heard his brother say over and over that, if given the chance, he would kill Bill Sherman in Jeff Davis' name.

Now, a Union soldier, hard-bitten by years of bloody campaigns, stood in front of Phil. Almost all of the rifles had been collected. Johnston had withdrawn his saber from its scabbard ready to hand it over to Sherman once the last rim-rifle repeater was in the wagons.

The Union soldier beckoned impatiently.

'Hand your fucking piece over, Reb. Be quick about it!'

Instead of obeying the order, Phil raised his rifle and took direct aim at Sherman. He, like Neil and others, had determined never to hand over an empty rifle. That would have been more than surrender, it would have been abject surrender.

Neil raised his own rifle in an effort to knock

Phil's weapon from his hands. 'No, no, no!' he shouted as he struggled to awaken.

It was always like that in his dream. His own rifle had fired and the shot struck his twin. Oh God! Again he heard that single shot, and again the sound was muffled as the lined-up Johnny Rebs burst into a rebel yell and a song. *Dixie*.

Neil was instantly free from slumber. How often would these terrifying nightmares plague him? He had no idea how long he had slept.

Dixie. He leaped from his bed. 'Dixie!' he shouted.

He flung open the door.

At the threshold, in the first light of Sunday's dawn, lay his beloved mustang.

Neil knew at once that he had heard a shot, a real shot not of his dreams, one that had put a bullet in Dixie's head.

A note, weighted by a stone, lay on the mustang's flank. With tears flooding his eyes, he knelt to read it.

Watch your hide, McAdam. You're next.

NINE

The first crimson streaks of dawn that Sunday morning crept above the crest of the far mountains as Neil arose finally from the side of Dixie. He sat on the earth between his dead mustang and the office door. He had let sorrow and his anger fight each other to a draw.

He recalled how he first spied Dixie in a corral near the Mexican border, and how he had coveted the mount at once. Dixie had broken away from the other horses and came trotting to him. The horse nickered and let him rub its nose and scratch behind its ears. 'You want me to spend my hard-earned dollars on you, don't you, boy?' Neil had whispered. 'Well, I need a horse to hold my saddle, and it looks like you need me.'

The mustang had then raised its head and neighed loud enough to make the Mexican *vaqueros* turn and stare.

'That's a rebel yell if I ever heard one,' Neil said, delighted at the mount's spirit. 'Guess I'd better call you Dixie.'

Neil sighed now as he stroked the back of the lifeless horse. He had known sadness often, but he had never felt like this before. The fading darkness did nothing to lighten his mourning. At the same time, he had never felt such anger. Rage formed a burning knot in his belly that wouldn't loosen.

'When I find the son of a bitch who did this I'll make him pay,' he vowed.

Hours had passed since he had found Dixie and the note with its grim warning, weighed down by a stone against the dead horse's flank. Now, as the sky began to flame with orange, someone approached on a horse. The sound of the hoofbeats broke into Neil's thoughts. Looking up, he waved a half-hearted welcome. Once again it was the crippled Brad Connors who arrived when Neil most needed a friend.

Connors wore a puzzled expression as he eyed the Benson manager. He lowered his glance to take in Dixie. He dismounted from Ginger his roan mare, and limped over to Neil.

Neil handed Connors the note of warning.

Connors swore. Then he put a hand on Neil's shoulder as he spoke. 'A few hours ago I dropped by Matt Felkins' house to talk about the meeting you called. Then I thought I'd drop in on you, but your office was dark. I heard a shot or something a lot like it. I went home and the thought kept hounding me like a beagle after a fox, considering someone shot at you a couple of weeks ago. I said to myself, "Brad, if you're so all-fired concerned go see what's up." So, here I am.'

Neil nodded.

'Want me to fetch Guy Rengert?'

'I don't need the sheriff.'

Neil went to the little lean-to at the rear of the office and got two shovels and a rope. He returned to Connors.

'I'd like to bury Dixie back there by those pines.

Dixie grazed there 'cause that was the only shady patch of grass.'

Neil made a lasso and drew it tight around Dixie's hind legs. He tossed the rope's other end to Connors. The crippled mine owner mounted Ginger and tied the rope around the saddle horn. He urged Ginger on and slowly pulled Neil's mustang to the small stand of pines.

'I want Dixie buried before full morning, Brad. That mustang was always full of mischief come morning.'

Connors nodded again.

Together, they dug until they managed a three-foot deep trench. They pulled Dixie into it. Neil began at once to shovel the dirt back over Dixie as if he couldn't wait to see his mustang laid to rest.

'Trouble seems to dog you, Neil.'

'I don't think it's me they're after. It's Miss Benson. that's why I called the meeting at her house this afternoon.'

'You're still having that get-together after this?' Connors pointed to the mustang's grave.

'I sure as hell am, friend.'

Neil smoothed out the mound to make it less obvious a grave. He broke off a small branch, then swept it over the path made from pulling Dixie to his burial site. He obliterated every trace of the sorrowful occurrence.

'I don't want nobody to know about this,' Neil said. 'Not a word. Folks'll find out soon enough, I reckon, maybe even afore I tell them. Maybe not. There are a few faces I want to watch at church.'

Neil told Connors about Tom Benson's desecrated marker and how Merle and he had scrubbed it clean and how he had returned it.

'If I see what I'm looking for, surprise mainly, then I'll want to ponder on it. If I can rein in my temper.' He offered his hand to Connors. 'Miss Benson will be along in a few hours to join me going to church.' He managed a weak smile. 'Womenfolk don't feel right unless they've gussied up a man and got him to Sunday meeting.'

'Want me to ride to Tom Benson's house and tell Miss Merle what's happened?'

'I'd sure be obliged. But only Miss Benson, none other.'

Connors nodded, mounted his horse, and then rode off.

As Neil dressed in his Sunday best, he told himself that he should banish thoughts of vengeance if he was heading for a spell at church. But his spirit wasn't up to it. He figured heaven would just have to put up with him and the way he felt.

He heard and recognized the gait of Merle's horse as she approached. He heard but did not recognize the hoofbeats of a second horse. He went to the office door and opened it to bright daylight. Merle, astride Firefly, held the reins of the second horse, a palomino. She was near to tears as she spoke.

'Oh, Neil, I'm so sorry. Brad came by and told me about Dixie.'

'I reckon whoever's behind the goings on are getting right serious, Merle.'

'How could anyone be so cruel?' She dismounted.

'I've seen men beat horses but I've never known a man to shoot one 'less it was the merciful thing to do.' Neil squinted at the rising sun. 'A man who'd shoot a horse is a dangerous man.'

'Do you have any idea as to who did it?'

'No, Merle, but I sure aim to find out.'

Grim-faced, he strapped on his holstered .44.

'Neil, you don't wear a gun to church!'

'Today, I do.' His voice was as dark as his words.

She sighed and nodded her acceptance of his mood. Then she brightened. She rubbed the palomino's nose.

'Neil, my father would want you to have this mount.' She handed Neil the reins of the palomino. 'Her name is Lady. She won't take the place of Dixie, but she's a good horse.'

'I never saw Tom ride her.'

'Oh, he did. But always alone. Daddy would ride out after sunset into the scrub and the foothills. He said he liked to think out things by himself. They were clearer that way with only Lady to nicker when it was time to ride home.' She mounted Firefly. 'He always called my mother Lady. That's where your palomino got her name.' She emphasized *your*.

An hour later they rode up to the little adobe church and the cemetery. Townspeople were gathered at the entrance. They chatted with one another and exchanged gossip. The women admired a new bonnet when they saw one. The men talked of silver mining and of horses. Yet, no one seemed to notice that Neil was not astride his mustang, Dixie. Neil studied faces but none appeared to betray a thought more serious than discomfort from being in his Sunday best. The women smelled of cedar chests and the men of witch hazel.

Neil noticed, too, that no one looking into the little graveyard seemed surprised that Tom

Benson's wooden marker was where it should be.

Parson Gabriel Ashe greeted the townspeople at the door. Hr frowned when he saw Neil's .44.

'Sorry, Brother McAdam, we can't welcome a firearm in a house of worship.'

'Preacher, from now on it goes with me on Sundays, too.'

'Not in church.'

'Then I'll wait outside and catch your words through an open window.' He handed Gabriel Ashe a dollar. 'That's for the collection.' As Neil turned away he thought he saw a "please" on Merle's lips, but he ignored it. Sometimes women didn't understand how men felt, how anger could burn like a branding iron against a man's soul. He turned away, too, from Amy Gentian who was giving him a schoolma'am frown. Women! He wanted to be beside Merle. He wanted also to force a showdown with someone who might betray his guilt, his cowardice, by wearing it on his face like an outlaw's mask.

He waited in vain.

Neil and Merle rode back to her house in silence. As they passed the Benson mine office, Neil refused to look at the jack pines where Dixie lay. He knew he would never forget the mustang, but he had a new horse now and he was determined to love Lady. He knew that if he did and showed it, the palomino would love him in return.

That afternoon, with Merle's usual chicken and dumplings Sunday dinner under his belt, Neil waited the arrival of the mine owners. He was elated at the turnout. Present, beside himself, Merle and their foreman, the nearly-recovered

Zack Meadows, were Harry and Millie Hawthorne, Matt and Rebecca Felkins, Lars and Ingrid Olsen, Brad Connors, his foreman Grant Tennant, and, to Neil's unfeigned surprise, Caleb Dunne. How had he got wind of the meeting?

Neil glanced at Connors who shook his head. Neil took this to mean that the crippled mine owner had kept his silence. Neil decided to tell the gathering about Tom Benson's despoiled grave marker, the shooting and death of Dixie, and the warnings he had received. Nothing could serve to point out more clearly the danger he and the others faced. Not only physical danger, but the even greater menace of losing all that they had worked so hard for.

There were expressions of surprise, shock, and then sympathy from the mine owners and their wives. Even from Caleb Dunne.

'Sure was a right fine animal, McAdam. Too bad.' Neil acknowledged Dunne's statement, but he was certain it was insincere. Still, he couldn't hold lack of sincerity against a man.

Merle left for the kitchen to make coffee and cut newly-baked apple pies for the group.

'Men, ladies, Miss Benson gave me leave to call this meeting. None of us need a spyglass to see that a lot of queer things have happened that shouldn't have. I think they're all related like cracker families back home.'

He pointed out that all the owners shared a great concern, but concern alone never got anything accomplished. Neil eyed the small gathering.

'Any comments?'

'I'm worried about my investment,' Felkins said. His wife, Rebecca, nodded.

'I fear for my family,' Olsen added. 'You all know my wife is expecting.' Ingrid Olsen put her hand on her swelling midriff as if to give credence to her husband's words.

'I figure someone's trying to scare us off out digs and then take over our holdings,' Hawthorne put in.

'Stuff and nonsense,' Dunne snorted. 'I'm not afraid, even though I've had my own troubles as you all know.'

'Maybe so, Mr Dunne,' Neil said, 'but I propose we form a Miners' Protective Association. We'll all look out for each other. Who here agrees an MPA is a good idea?'

Dunne smiled as if the chorus of 'ayes' amused him. Then he changed his smile to an expression of patience as if he were dealing with recalcitrant school children.

'We don't need a Miners' Protective Association, folks. Looks too much like we're all suspicious of one another. Not me. If you're worried, I'm not. I once heard Doc Whitman say that I'm rapacious. Trust those educated critters – though I don't think Doc can boast of much in the way of education – to use two-bit words. He could've come right out and called me greedy. I'm not. Now, it's no crime to be rich, but it helps.'

'You got rich,' Hawthorne cried out, 'by latching on to your brother's share in the Gila.'

'If he hadn't been murdered, his share wouldn't have come my way.' Dunne's complexion reddened with his sudden anger.

'We all know how you felt about Howie,' Olsen said in a placatory voice.

'Thank you, Olsen. Now if any of you are willing,

I'm agreeable to buying some or all of your holdings.'

'Forget it!' Hawthorne shouted, his red face growing redder.

'Never!' Felkins scowled. His sandy moustache followed the scornful curve of his lips.

'I'll never sell my digs!' Connors exclaimed.

'I'll stand by you boss.' Grant Tennant stuttered as he spoke.

'You'll all be sorry!' Dunne shouted.

'Not I, Caleb,' broke in Lars Olsen, his arm around his wife. 'I'll accept your offer. My crew is leaving as it is.'

Expressions of outrage filled the parlour at Olsen's knuckling under. Neil tried to calm Olsen and the others. 'Looks like we do need an MPA. We've got to stick together.' Then his own anger leaped out of control as Dunne, sneering, took him by the shoulder and spun him around.

'How about you, McAdam? I'll buy your 35 per cent of the Benson digs. Name your price.'

'It ain't for sale.'

'Everything in the world's for sale.' Dunne's sneer grew uglier. 'Or are you aiming to add Merle Benson's 65 per cent to what you've already talked her out of since old Tom died?'

Enraged, Neil lunged at Dunne. He drove his left fist into the Gila owner's nose. He smashed his right fist into Dunne's mouth. Blood spurted from both nose and mouth. As the mine owner reeled back and fell, the women present screamed.

'I don't aim to fight a man near twice my age, Mr Dunne, but you need your mouth washed out.' Neil moved to help Dunne to his feet, but Hawthorne and Felkins held him back.

'Easy, Neil, let him go!'

Dunne staggered to his feet. He kept his distance, but he shook his fist and cursed Neil. 'You think you're so all-fired smart, don't you, you nosey southern snot? Well, you better keep an eye over your shoulder, kid, and don't sit with your back to a window.'

With that, Dunne stumbled out of the Bensons' house.

Neil faced the quiet mine owners and shook his head at what his temper had cost him. Merle came in from the kitchen. She carried a tray with plates of pie and mugs of coffee. She seemed to sense at once that the tension in the room was thick as a sudden sand storm in the desert.

Neil knew he wasn't all-fired smart. He was only sure that he was all-fired right about the need for banding together, the need for a protective association. He was also certain, MPA or not, that their *real* troubles had just begun.

TEN

Despite Caleb Dunne's threats against Neil, a week passed without any further trouble. However, Neil had never once let his guard down. Work at the Benson mine proceeded on schedule and as far as he knew work went along smoothly at the other mines on the Apache Bend mother lode.

The only non-productive silver mine at the moment was Lars Olsen's digs. Despite the urging of the other mine owners, Olsen refused to change his decision to sell out to Dunne. Everyone knew that Olsen was a good man who was cowed by Dunne and who would listen and accede to the wishes of his wife, Ingrid. The womenfolk could understand Ingrid's feelings and fears. She was with child and naturally she was concerned about the mine disasters. If she wished to leave Apache Bend, who could fault her?

On the Saturday following the attack upon Dunne by Neil, the young manager of the Benson mine decided to become better acquainted with Tom Benson's horse, the palomino Lady. He would teach Lady the tricks he had taught Dixie. He would train Lady to come to him when he whistled. He would show her how to stand calm when he leaped into the saddle by putting both

hands on her rump and leaping over her tail, or by
swinging into the saddle without using a stirrup.
He was sure that was something Tom Benson had
not been able to do.

There was one thing that Tom Benson did
before he was murdered, and that was to take long
rides into the desert at twilight. Merle had said that
her father would lope along, easy-like, his hands
ever so loose on the reins, letting Lady blaze her
own trail. That, Merle's father had said, was the
way a man could think on things best.

Neil knew he had a lot to ponder. On that
Saturday, July 12th, at twilight, Neil saddled Lady
and rode her north of the town, then headed west
on a line parallel to but well south of the Gila.

Sand formed a carpet that was spread before the
foothills. Cactus stood, arms upraised, silent
sentinels in the night that neither barred his way or
challenged him with a 'who goes there?' as sentinels
had so often in the past, when he was a Johnny
Reb.

Neil knew that ahead, over the low mountain
range, was the broad valley through which the Gila
flowed. Sometimes it was sand-clogged and
sluggish, at other times it raged through the valley
when sudden cloudbursts swelled the waterway as
it coursed for 500 miles until it was swallowed by
the great Colorado. Some day, he promised
himself, he would travel its westward path to see
the tumbling river that had carved out the big
canyon.

Now, he was content, as Tom Benson had been,
to let Lady choose her path. He wondered if, by
habit, she was loping along the same trail over
which she had carried Benson. He liked to think it

was so. It made him feel closer than ever to his benefactor.

'Tom,' he said half aloud, 'I figure you know I took your grave marker back to where it belonged. Whoever defaced and moved it made me madder than a drone that the queen bee wouldn't let back in the skep. But a drone's fate is nature, don't aim to quarrel with that, but what that mean skunk did to your grave is against all nature. Can't figure out who'd do that. I'll need to ponder.'

A few moments later he halted Lady. He dismounted and sat down near a clump of sagebrush.

Neil lay back and pillowed his head in his hands. Darkness had come upon the desert quickly despite the fact that it was summer and that the longest day was less than a month earlier. The stars in a cloudless sky twinkled like the diamonds in the nursery rhyme he remembered his mother reading to him and Phil so long ago. And, as in the nursery rhyme, he wondered what the stars were now and what they had been for hundreds of years and what happened when one fell. Somewhere up there was a lucky star, his alone, for it had brought him to Merle.

He remembered that first kiss a week ago on the porch of her home, and the kisses that followed during the past few days. The kisses were warm on their lips, and as they became more frequent they betokened a more ardent passion to come. His feelings for Merle grew stronger by the hour. He wanted to speed up his courtship of her but he hesitated asking her to marry him when his life was in jeopardy from some unknown source.

He traced the path of stars that outlined the big

dipper. What a powerful lot of water it would hold, maybe enough to fill the oceans to the west and east that he had never seen. There was so much he had never seen, and so much that he had.

'Tom,' he said aloud, loud enough to cause Lady to turn and gaze at him. 'Tom, you were the finest man, save my father, I ever knew. You trusted me and asked no questions. I remember you telling me a man's past is his past, that what counts is today. Now that I aim to ask Merle to marry me, don't know when, what counts is tomorrow.' He turned his palomino. 'Lady, you tell me what tomorrow brings.'

He sat up and ran his fingers through his blond hair. He shook the sand from it. Who knew, certainly not a palomino, what tomorrow would bring? He was grateful that, through his years of wandering, he never knew on one day what the next day promised. Perhaps that was just as well. He had enough companions riding with him, guilt and grief, that he didn't need another one named uncertainty to hop on his shoulders.

He felt he had finally left his past when he arrived at Apache Bend. But had he? Caleb Dunne's reference to a bounty hunter up north still caused a tightening in his gut. Had Dunne known more than he'd admitted? Was the reference only to Dunne's desire to get Sheriff Guy Rengert to put a bounty hunter on the trail of Joel Dunne?

The few times Neil had met Joel he had been impressed with the clean-cut son of Howard Dunne. He found it nigh impossible to believe that young Joel, just a kid really, could have murdered his own father. But Joel's uncle, Caleb, swore that he had found the boy standing, with a smoking gun, over the body of Howard Dunne. When a gun smokes, chances are it's just been fired. Neil sighed and stood. Seemed like whoever was connected with Caleb Dunne found himself sooner or later in trouble.

He mounted the palomino. 'Come on, Lady, let's head for home.'

That same Saturday afternoon, Dunne surveyed the wall map in his office. He circled his own mine, the Gila, then he circled the newly-acquired digs of Lars Olsen. He drew a line between them. One down, four to go. Of course the deal with Olsen hadn't been finalized yet and he had no doubt that the other mine owners would try to pressure Olsen to change his mind. He felt assured that Olsen was too cowed to take back his offer to sell. That and the fact that Olsen's wife would make sure she and Lars would pull up stakes in Apache Bend.

Dunne jabbed his finger at the site of the Benson mine on the wall map. That was the digs he coveted the most. Merle Benson didn't stand in his way. Neil McAdam did. Dunne rubbed his swollen mouth. McAdam would pay for that. No man humiliated Dunne in front of others.

He heard hoofbeats outside his office. In a moment Sheriff Rengert entered the Gila office.

'You sent for me, Mr Dunne? Hey I heard about McAdam and you.'

'I did, and you heard lies.'

'What do you want?'

'News, you idiot!' Dunne enjoyed the sheriff's discomfiture at being addressed in that fashion. 'I want news. Have you any leads on the whereabouts of my nephew, Joel? The kid's been gone two months now and you haven't done a fucking thing during those two months to find him, to bring him to justice.'

'If we nab him, Mr Dunne, it'll be his word against yours.'

Dunne sneered and his eyes narrowed. 'Who do you think a jury'll believe? A kid who shot his father? Or me, a respected citizen of Apache Bend and Arizona Territory?' He turned to the wall map and put his finger on the Gila's site. 'If my nephew goes free he'll inherit my brother's share of the mine. Right now Howard's share belongs to me! I swear no murdering kin of mine will get it!' Dunne's dark features turned livid. 'Find him, Rengert, or I'll have your fucking badge!'

On that same Saturday a determined rider, always heading southward through the territory, stopping at every town, every isolated adobe ranch and sod-house farm, kept asking the same question to all who gave him heed. 'Have you seen this man? Name of Neil McAdam. Here's his picture. Have you seen him?'

Upon his return from his evening and night ride into the desert, Neil tethered Lady, removed her saddle, rubbed her down, and then threw a blanket across her back. It was nearing midnight when, after mulling over the mine's records, he snuffed out the lamp and turned in. His last thought before drifting into sleep was a hope that the nightmare of Johnston's surrender to Sherman would not return.

He woke a few hours before dawn. He was grateful that the nightmare was not the cause.

What then? He was sure he heard a noise beyond the door? Footsteps? He arose quietly and dressed in the dark. Before stepping out of his office to investigate he strapped on his .44. He raced in a zig-zag pattern to the mine's entrance. He saw a figure run out of the mine tunnel. Neil halted to bring the fleeing individual into focus. Too late. The trespasser mounted a horse in the darkness. The sound of hoofbeats faded from earshot.

Neil approached the mine tunnel with cautious steps. If there were others there who had no business on the Benson site, he wanted to surprise them.

It was Neil who was surprised. The blast from a tremendous explosion rocked the tunnel. Neil found himself, eardrums ringing and stabbed by pain, flat on his back. He was conscious of only one thing. The big dipper he had traced earlier that night had tipped and was pouring stars all over him.

ELEVEN

Neil wondered if, by some careless misstep, he had fallen into the Apache Bend stamping mill, and that his head, like ore rock, was being crushed in the expectation of finding silver.

As if she were at the far end of the main tunnel in the Benson mine, Merle's voice came to him in waves. Shock waves.

'Sunday morning,' she murmured. 'Everything seems to happen on Sunday morning.'

'Probably Old Nick.' It was a man's voice. 'Wants to make sure he does his mischief on the one day folks get set to go to church.'

'Will he be all right, Doctor?'

'I suspect so. He's young, hardy, always manages to take his lumps,' Doc Whitman replied.

Neil could not recollect what happened after the blast in the Benson digs. Merle said it was Sunday, so that would make it just a few hours since he left the mine office, gun in hand, to investigate something – what? – in the mine itself.

He made a great inner effort to shake off the lead weights that prevented him from opening his eyes. He willed the weights to fall from his face, Finally, when he could gaze about him, he discovered that there had been no lead ore on his eyelids at all. He almost wished there had been because the bright daylight jabbed cactus fingers in his eyes. He moaned, closed his eyelids for a moment, then slowly opened them again.

He was in a strange room. Merle stood at his side, with her hand on his brow. Doc Whitman was at the foot of the bed, and beyond him, near the door, stood a cluster of people whose blurred faces advanced toward him, then fell back. Advance, retreat. Who were they?

'Am I in a hospital?' Neil whispered.

'No,' Doc Whitman obliged.

'You're in my house, Neil,' Merle added. 'Brad Connors found you by the mine and brought you here.'

'Then I fetched the old Doc,' Connors said, his face drifting in and out. The voice was recognizable but his features were not.

Neil remembered that the crippled mine owner always appeared on the scene when he was most needed. He sure was in debt to Brad many times over.

'Thanks,' he whispered.

During the next half hour Neil became more aware of his surroundings. He took a few sips of water to irrigate the desert that filled his throat. Although his head still felt crushed, his eyesight had sharpened and the faces of those in the room held steady. Besides Doc Whitman and Merle, there were Connors, Lars and Ingrid Olsen, the foreman, Zack Meadows, and the pretty school ma'am, Amy Gentian.

'What happened?' Neil asked, his voice growing stronger.

'Don't know for sure, boss,' Zack said. 'We'll find

out though.'

'You've had a slight concussion, Neil, still it's nothing to be treated lightly. Have to keep an eye on you, son.'

'No, sir, Doc. I've got to get back to the mine and the office.'

'Confound it, McAdam, you've got to get better first! You're staying put!'

Neil did not reply with words, he tried action. He struggled to sit up and the room spun around like the wooden tops he and his twin brother played with as young boys. He sank back on the feather pillow.

He guessed he was in Tom Benson's bedroom. Merle had told him that the room had been left untouched since her father's death. Neil rested on Tom Benson's large, comfortable oak bed, and wherever he looked he saw reflections of Mr and Mrs Benson's life. There were shelves of books that Merle's father and mother had cherished. He couldn't read the titles from where he lay, but Merle had told him about some of them, *The Pathfinder, The Last of the Mohicans, Moby Dick, The House of the Seven Gables* and others. Merle smiled at him.

'I see you're looking at daddy's books,' she said. 'He loved to read. He wanted to name me Eva, after Little Eva in *Uncle Tom's Cabin*, but mother wouldn't let him.'

'Lucky you weren't named Topsy,' Amy Gentian said, giggling.

Neil, from Georgia, was unaware of *Uncle Tom's Cabin*, but at that moment Neil determined to read every one of Tom Benson's books if it took him a lifetime. He wanted to be as much like Tom as he could.

Neil spotted a graceful rocking chair that must

have been Mrs Benson's. Nearby was a sturdier rocker placed by the window. Next to it, on a small table, was Tom's pipe and humidor. Well, maybe he'd take up a pipe, too, and try out Tom's tobacco if Merle would let him.

On a nightstand by the bed was a framed ferrotype of Merle. Wait! Not Merle. It was the image of someone very like Merle. She saw him staring at it.

'My mother, taken just before she died.'

'She was beautiful,' Neil said.

Brad Connors brought everyone in the room back to the import of the moment. 'Got any idea what caused the explosion, Neil?'

'Probably dynamite.'

Brad limped over to the bed. 'You know what I mean, McAdam. You got any idea *who* might of done it?'

Neil shook his head and the effort brought forth a low moan.

'No idea, Brad. Someone who fires at people in the dark, who sends wagons smashing into offices, who desecrates a grave, who shoots horses!' Neil's voice rose with his anger and he tried to sit up again. Doc Whitman's hand eased him back on the pillow.

'Easy, Neil.'

Ingrid Olsen, heavy with child, came alongside Merle.

'You see, Merle, you see what's happening?' she asked in thick Swedish accents. 'I think you should sell your mine. Caleb Dunne's a good man. He'll give you a fair price.'

Merle's eyes flashed defiance. 'Absolutely not!'

Neil realized anew what a spunky girl she was.

'Enough talk of selling,' Connors said.

'It's easy to be brave when you're a man,' Ingrid said. 'All the owners are except you, Merle. A girl can't go it alone. Lars is selling only because of the little one we're expecting.'

'True, they're all men,' Merle replied. 'But Neil represents me and he's man enough for the job.'

Neil heard a loud knocking at the front door and he saw Amy Gentian leave to answer it. She returned with Ned Lockhart, the husky crew member who worked under Zack Meadows.

'Look what I found, boss!' He held up three short lengths of fuse. 'Somebody made a bunch of dynamite bombs and planted them in the tunnel and the main shaft. Whoever it was left in a hurry and didn't pick up his leavings.'

'How much damage?' Zack asked.

'Looks like a herd of buffalo roared through the mine.' Then, noticing he was in the presence of three ladies, Ned took off his cap. 'Sorry to bear such bad news, ma'am,' he said to Merle.

'Now, that's enough of this talk!' Doc Whitman raised his hand. 'Clear out, all of you. Go home, do something, go to church. McAdam has got to rest and sleep. Trouble dogs this boy like a wolf tracks sheep. Now, scoot!'

The Olsens, Brad, Zack and Ned, turned to leave, whispering encouraging words to Neil and Merle as they departed.

'Now, McAdam, you're to spend the next few days here.'

'Of course he will, doctor,' Merle agreed.

Amy Gentian smiled. 'Just so the town gossips won't have any fat to chew on, I'll stay with you, Merle, and help you keep an eye on Neil.'

Doc Whitman closed his bag. 'You're in good hands, McAdam. Can you manage to stay intact for at least a week?' He turned to Merle. 'See that he rests. Don't feed him too much. Keep cool damp cloths on his forehead. I'll look in tomorrow.'

The two young women followed the doctor to the parlor.

Neil stared at Tom Benson's books. For a moment he felt as if the late mine owner was sitting there in his rocker, watching.

'Doggone it, Tom,' he whispered, 'it's gonna take some time to dig out your mine.' Neil's heart sank as he addressed the rocker. 'I was counting on selling your yield to an agent of the U.S. Mint for silver dollars. I promised your girl I'd do that.'

Neil mulled over the unsettling events of the past month. Somewhere there was a pattern he had to find. Was wealthy Caleb Dunne's greed behind it all? No, for Dunne had his own problems. Two questions chased each other in Neil's mind. Was the Gila mine cave-in planned by Dunne to throw off suspicion by others? And who in the devil was trying to kill him? The questions remained unanswered and shortly he drifted off into a troubled sleep.

Within two days, Neil recovered from the slight concussion. He moved back into his quarters in the Benson mine office where he could keep a closer eye on things. The next three weeks he and his crew were busy working twelve hours a day to clear the mine from the rocks, timbers, twisted rails, ore cars and debris that were left following the explosion.

'Back-breaking work, huh, boss?' Zack Meadows grunted.

Neil acknowledged the truth of his foreman's appraisal. 'Sure tougher'n I figured, Zack.'

The other mine owners, except Caleb Dunne, sent members of their crews to lend a hand, just as they had several weeks earlier when Harry Hawthorne suffered the blast at his mine.

Hawthorne spoke up. 'Any idea who'd do this to me and now to you? The sheriff come up with anything?'

'Rengert couldn't find his shadow on a sunny day,' Neil replied.

Hawthorne ran a hand through his dark hair. The one-time, red-faced Indian fighter scowled. 'Speaking of shadows, Neil, I've seen someone lurking around my digs at night, moves so fast I can't pin him down. Matt Felkin says he's spied some shadowy figure, too, thin as a sapling, but whoever it is melts into the darkness.'

'Maybe a thief?'

'Don't know, Neil. Sometimes Matt and me get the idea that whoever it is wants to be caught. Don't seem like a thief to me.'

Wants to be caught? Neil shook his head. He didn't believe that anyone who had done something wrong, who was fleeing from – from what? – would want to be caught. Was he thinking of some mysterious figure who melts into the darkness? Or was he thinking of himself?

TWELVE

On Saturday, August 2nd, just three weeks after the dynamite blast, Neil and the crews finished putting the Benson mine back in operating condition. Neil thanked the men sent over by other mine owners, and promised they'd be well-paid by Miss Benson.

Neil had seen little of Merle during the past three weeks. When she did come to her mine to see the progress of the crews, Neil couldn't show his affection for her. He wanted to hold her and kiss her and declare himself, but always there was someone present. But now the work was finished.

'Tonight, Merle, we're going to ride out to where everything is peaceful.'

Neil on Lady and Merle on Firefly skirted Apache Bend and rode into the high desert and the foothills of the Gila range. Neil was happy riding for miles along deserted, quiet trails. He loved the night sky that shoved aside the sunset. He marvelled at the bright stars that studded the heavens.

They came to a clump of pines that grew in the midst of the sand and dirt and rocks. Neil grinned, for actually it was Lady that led them to the spot. She, like Dixie before her, liked to graze on the tender grass shoots beneath the pines.

Wind-driven clouds from the northwest began to erase the stars. A sudden coolness touched their faces, more than normal for evenings at the start of August, and a scent of rain was in the air. Then, lightning lit up the area where they sat.

The two horses huddled together and nickered softly.

'Reckon we better head for your house, Merle. Storm's due.'

'Let it storm. I want to have my face in the wind and rain. I want you to shelter me.'

He put his arms around her. 'But you'll want real shelter. Let me show you how I lived on the plains and desert before your father took me on. I've built many a lean-to, I've lived off the land.'

He went to his saddle bags and Lady eyed him with curiosity as he took from one a hatchet, a Bowie knife, a length of rope, a canteen filled with water, two tinplate pots, two each of tinplate dishes and cups, and two each of forks and spoons. From the other, he took a can of condensed milk, a packet of ground coffee, some strips of jerky, two cans of baked beans, and two pieces of hardtack.

He eyed the sky, lit up by flashes of lightning, and he quickened his steps to the center of the grove of pines. There he sought out the smallest of trees, new growth not much taller than himself. He selected branches two inches in diameter and trunks three inches across. He chopped them down quickly and carried them back to where Merle waited. He stripped off small twigs and knurls with his knife.

He cut two of the thicker limbs in six foot lengths and then set them upright in the dirt six feet apart.

He notched the top ends of the two uprights and then laid a seven foot branch across the width that separated them. Next, he sloped branches, each seven feet long, from the limb that spanned the uprights to the ground. He tied all the branches together with short lengths of rope. Finally, he piled small branches with the pine needles still on them across the sloping top and against the sides. He bound everything together with rope.

That finished, he lined the ground beneath the lean-to with short twigs of pine needles to make a soft, comfortable bed. He untied two blanket rolls from where they rested across Lady's back behind his saddle, then put them atop the pine needle layer in the shelter.

'That oughtta do for easing a body,' he told himself. 'At least for me. I hope for Merle, too.' He turned to her and spoke aloud. 'Oughtta shelter us, but if it rains hard it'll probably leak like a bucket used for target practice. If we hurry we might get a supper going afore a storm rises.'

'You may have fended for yourself on the trail,' Merle said, 'but let me handle supper, Neil.'

'I know you're a right fine cook, but ain't much you can do with what we've got here.'

'We'll see,' she said. 'While I get things ready, you can build a fire.'

He bent to the task, gathering a few pine chips, twigs and small branches. He arranged them in the shape of a slender cone. Then he drove two stout forked sticks, each about two feet high, into the dirt, one on each side of the cone. He lit the little makeshift pyre in several places. Then he fed the blaze with more chips and twigs and pieces of small branches. He fanned the fire with his hat. Satisfied,

Neil laid another green branch in the forks of the uprights so that it straddled the blaze.

He turned his attention to Merle. She had been busy preparing the meal in the darkness, but now she had the light of the fire as well as the lightning to let her see what she was doing. She had cut lengths of sun dried beef into small pieces and had placed them in one of the tinplate pots. She filled the other with water in which she emptied the packet of coffee.

'Please open the can of milk and the two cans of beans,' she asked.

She handed him the Bowie knife and he punctured the can of milk. Then he used the blade as a can opener to get at the beans. Merle covered the jerky in the pot with the baked beans. She hung the pot over the fire. She did the same with the pot of water and coffee. She stirred the beans and jerky. Once the coffee boiled, she let the grounds settle before filling the cups and adding milk. When the beans simmered she filled the plates. She added hardtack.

'I fear our meal is very primitive, Neil,' she said, 'but it's the best I can do with what we have.'

The aroma of the bubbling mixture of beans and jerky tantalized his nostrils. When he tasted her improvised stew he found the flavor had not let the aroma down. A draw, sure as hell. He dipped his hard tack in the coffee. He gave a sigh that signaled contentment.

'I fear, too,' he said, echoing her apologetic note, 'that you've served up a meal fit for a potentate.'

'Neil, you don't know what a potentate is.'

A vagrant thought blew in on the winds of the gathering storm. 'A critter like Caleb Dunne,' he said, giving voice to the thought.

'He's probably a very decent man,' Merle said.

'Well, he harbors no love for his nephew Joel.'

'Do you think Joel Dunne shot his father? Killed him?'

'I just don't know.' He amended that. 'I don't think so.'

He finished his plate of beans and jerky. 'This I do think, Merle. There's no better cook in Arizona Territory.'

'Thank you. a woman does her best cooking when she has a man to cook for.' She smiled at Neil, a smile that the fire made even brighter. 'My mother told me that the day she first showed me how to make buttermilk biscuits.'

She rose, took the plates, cups, pans, forks and spoons, and then cleansed them by adding water and sand and scouring them with leaves.

He watched her, admiring her slim, firm body and lithe movements. She was as graceful as a doe in the forest. He had marveled at her many times, always telling himself that she was the owner of the Benson digs and reminding his eager eyes that he was her employee.

She turned. Still smiling, she sat beside him. 'You've never really told me about yourself, Neil. Isn't it about time?'

Good God, had she divined his thoughts? How could he tell her why he left Georgia and the devastation left by General Sherman? Would she believe him? What words could he find to explain why he had wandered ever westward for years, why his heart stopped every time there was word of a bounty hunter? How do you phrase an answer that indicated *there's nothing to much to tell, my darling, I'm just a murderer, anything else you want to know?*

At that moment the rains came.

Torrential sheets of water driven by the wind swept over them. It was as if the cloudburst had been conceived in crashing thunder and jagged lightning and was now ripped from the womb of fury. Neil stood, then grasped her by the arms and raised her to her feet. He carried her into his lean-to. The rain beat against the shelter's rear slope creating a small waterfall. The front opening was on the lee side of the wind and although water sprayed them, most of the rain was swept away. Unlike his earlier prophecy, Neil noted the lean-to did not leak like a bucket used for target practice. He had not lost his skill.

The fire, giving no battle, had been vanquished by the rain. So had their canopy of stars. Over his shoulder, as lightning flashed, Neil could just make out Lady and Firefly. They had retreated further into the clump of pines.

'You wanted me to shelter you, Merle,' he teased, 'and so I have.' He saw her shiver. Good God, what was he thinking? they had to dry their clothes as best they could. They had to get warm.

'We're as wet as a bath on Saturday night,' he said. 'I'll turn my back so that you can shed your wet togs and get under a blanket. Then you do the same for me while I strip.'

'Neil, for heaven's sake, I'm not a prude, so don't you be. Why turn our backs? Besides, it's dark as a mine shaft.'

True. He grinned in the blackness. Was there ever a woman as unpredictable as Merle Benson?

They took off their clothes in less than a minute,

and in less time than that they were under blankets.
They clung to each other, their naked wet bodies
were joined as if by an adhesive made from desire
on his part and passion on hers. He found her lips
with his hungry own. He knew at once that this was
a kiss unlike any he had ever known. Every glimpse
of Merle in the past, every longing look at her,
concealed as best as he could manage, was now a
fulfilled promise.

His few words of endearment were drowned by
the pelting of the rain on the boughs above them.
An occasional lightning flash made her face visible.
She was wide-eyed, her face shone with ectasy. His
hands explored her rounded breasts and lithe
body, her palms traced his muscular chest and flat
belly.

Their bodies grew warm under the blankets. He
cradled her head on his left shoulder and placed
his left hand across the hardened nipples of her
breasts. He moved his right hand to her navel and
then continued his movement downward. Slow,
teasing. She didn't protest. She parted her slim
legs. He turned to her as she turned to him. She
guided his manhood into the moist warmth of her
body.

'Oh, Neil, Neil,' she moaned. There was a
moment when a barrier blocked his penetration,
then he broke through. He heard her slight scream
above the storm.

The elements of nature still raged outside the
lean-to. Inside, the raging elements of human
nature enfolded their bodies and Neil no longer
was conscious of thunder or of lightning or of rain,
but only of that moment when he exploded within
her. His lips sought hers. He knew that there were

only two people in the great wide world, and that they were here in the shelter he had made for his beloved. The scent of pine mingled with the aroma of sex.

After a few moments she whispered 'my darling,' then held him close. After several minutes he murmured, 'I love you, Merle.' She did not respond. He sensed that the thunder had rolled off into the distance and that the rain had thinned. 'I love you, Merle,' he repeated. Again no response except for her gentle breathing.

'Well, I'm damned,' he muttered to himself, 'she's asleep.' Where had he heard that it was usually the man who, spent, rolled over and slumbered?

'I aim to marry you, girl,' he whispered to the night, 'but how can I keep from hurting you?' Were he to ask for her hand would she accept? Or, would she settle for this night of love and keep her distance in the morning? Be boss lady again? Would she think he really wanted to take over the Benson mine? He would make sure she knew he had no such intentions. How could he explain his past? How could he explain away the bounty hunter?

The questions dogged him until he, too, fell asleep.

When they awoke in the morning the rain was gone, the air was fresh, and the sun was high. The mud had begun to dry. Their clothes, though still damp, would dry as they rode back to Merle's house.

He crawled from the lean-to. Something caught his attention. A few yards from the shelter, footprints, not their own, were embedded in the drying mud. A set of strange boots had approached, paused and waited, then walked away. If either Lady or Firefly had neighed a warning, he had not heard it.

He did not point out the bootprints to Merle. But as they rode back to Apache Bend, he could not dispel his thoughts. Who had been stalking them? Who had watched them sleep? Who chose not to reveal himself? And just as important as who – *why*?

THIRTEEN

No matter how long or how hard he concentrated on the events that had plagued the mine owners in the previous weeks, he could not fit the pieces of the puzzle together. His brother Phil had been good at jigsaw puzzles. Neil, outlining borders, always had a difficult time filling the center. Discovering the bootprints of a stranger who had spent time watching Merle and himself while they slept in the lean-to, didn't make puzzle-solving any easier.

Why had no harm come to them from whoever had trailed them and then held back? If they had not been in danger, why didn't the nighttime visitor come forward and show himself?

After considerable thought, Neil came to the conclusion that the puzzling things that had occurred were directed primarily against Merle. She was the lone woman in the group of six mine owners and someone obviously considered her weak.

It was fortunate that so far only the Olsens, and certainly not Merle, had been badgered into selling. Lars and Ingrid were planning to pull stakes from Apache Bend within a month.

'We go east,' Ingrid said. 'I do not want our child

born in the center of violence.'

Merle was as defiant as the remaining mine owners, with the exception of Caleb Dunne who was in the position of buying, not selling. Whoever was behind it all must realize that Merle was of the same mettle as her late father.

Neil's head ached from his pondering.

A week after his and Merle's return from the pine grove, Neil knew it was time to call another meeting of the Miners' Protective Association.

As before, Merle agreed to the use of her parlor. Harry and Millie Hawthorne were there, as were Matt and Rebecca Felkins and Brad Connors. To Neil's amazement, more than surprise, Caleb Dunne made an appearance. Neil really didn't expect Lars Olsen to show up, but at the last minute the mine owner joined them.

'You sold out yet, Olsen?' Hawthorne demanded.

Olsen shifted his pale eyes from Hawthorne to Dunne, then moved his uneasy glance back to Hawthorne.

'Ain't no money changed hands yet, Harry. Hoping for it soon.'

'You'll get your blamed money!' Dunne thundered.

Merle said she would keep minutes of the MPA meeting and duly noted that it was held on Sunday afternoon, August 9th, 1873. She apologized for not having notes covering the first meeting but since the most important thing that happened then was the unfortunate incident involving Mr Dunne, and since everybody knew about it anyway, what was the point?

'Not quite so, Miss Benson,' Neil said good-naturedly. 'Since our last meeting, your mine got dynamited. I was a pretty lucky man not to have been injured more than I was.'

Dunne sneered as he spoke: 'Looks to me like Miss Benson took good care of you – in more ways than one.'

Anger flared in Millie Hawthorne's eyes. 'You should be ashamed of yourself, Mr Dunne. That remark is unworthy of you!'

'Maybe it wasn't,' Rebecca Felkins said. 'I've never noticed Mr Dunne given to right good manners.'

'Apologize!' the crippled Connors demanded.

'Who to, McAdam? Why in the devil should I?' Dunne asked.

'Not to Neil, to Miss Benson,' Hawthorne directed.

A moment of silence passed before Dunne turned to Merle and nodded so slightly it was barely noticeable. His one word was curt and almost inaudible.

'Sorry.'

'Let's get on with the meeting,' Neil said, hoping that his own relief at escaping a Donnybrook did not show too much. He was not afraid to fight and he wouldn't pick one himself, he was certain Merle knew that, but the business of the MPA was more important.

'We've got to try and come up with some ideas on how to protect ourselves. We've got to stick together closer than a dish of chili sticks to your ribs on a cold day,' Neil stated.

'What for?' Dunne put in. 'You're all acting like a bunch of lily-livered owners that can't protect your holdings by yourselves. Well I can, men. I don't need no fool MPA to stand guard for me. That's why I'm not running from a spot of trouble that ain't worth spit.' He acted as if he was about to do just that when, exercising some good manners to prove Rebecca Felkins wrong, he refrained from soiling Merle Benson's neatly-kept parlor.

'No I ain't aiming to run from trouble even though, like you all know, I've had my share of it myself,' Dunne went on. 'When I've got a problem, I put the sheriff on it. that's what a man of the law is for.'

'Like the way Guy Rengert ain't found your nephew, Josh, yet?' Connors asked.

'Rengert couldn't find the lockup if it didn't have a light in the window,' Matt Felkins said.

'Listen, men, the sheriff's working on it,' Dunne said. 'Now if you can't handle your digs by yourself or with someone else, maybe being a silver miner ain't up your alley. That's the only reason I'm offering to buy your holdings. I don't want to see my neighbours stranded high and dry.'

'Please, everybody, let's get on with the meeting,' Neil urged, as politely as he could in the presence of Dunne.

Dunne stepped forth to address the little MPA group.

'You fools!' he shouted. 'My offer still stands. Name your price, I'll meet it. But not for long.'

'I think you better leave, Dunne,' Neil said. There was no threat in his voice. 'No one here, 'cepting Lars Olsen, is listening to you.'

Dunne turned to Neil. His features were distorted with his anger.

'Pretty brave, ain't you, boy? If I were you I'd get

off your high horse. I hear there's a bounty hunter up at Gila crossing asking questions about someone who could be you. If I were you, I'd let Miss Benson make her own decisions. If I were you, boy, I'd shake the dust of Apache Bend off my boot heels and clear out of town. Go back where you came from. Reb!'

With that, Caleb Dunne stormed out.

Neil saw that everyone in the room, except Merle, was regarding him with deep concern clouding their eyes.

Bounty hunter? What the hell – had his past almost caught up with him at last?

The next morning, a Monday, Dieter Koesler rode up on his aging palomino to Brad Connors' mine office. The mine was in full operation and Koesler regarded the activity on the outside with interest. He started the conversation in a friendly tone which raised suspicion in Brad's mind at once. Connors decided to see what would happen.

'How's the leg, Mr Connors?' Koesler asked in his guttural German accents.

'Fair. Can't complain. What do you want?' Connors responded and asked his question in a voice that sounded very tired. He ran his hand through his graying hair.

'Came to give you the good wishes of my boss.'

'Don't need Dunne's good wishes, Koesler.' Bowed by his years of struggle and hardship, Connors made an effort to stand tall and straighten his shoulders.

'Mr Dunne figures a man of good sense you are, not like the others. Like he said, he would like you to name your price and he will add a thousand dollars to it. What say you?'

'I say get the devil off my digs. I'm loyal to the MPA. Tell your boss a flat no. Now, *vamos*.'

'I think you will be sorry.' Koesler swung back on his horse and rode off.

Ten minutes later, down the road, around the bend and out-of-sight of the Connors' mine and office, Koesler encountered Grant Tennant. Brad's foreman was heading for the mine. Koesler saw that he had been recognized and that Tennant had turned his mount so as to block the Gila foreman's way.

'What are you doing ... on Mr Connors' property?' Tennant stammered as he asked the question. 'Now clear the hell outta here unless you want to dance ... to a few bullets.' Tennant drew his gun.

At that warning, Koesler pulled his own gun.

A half hour after Koesler's departure, Brad Connors heard hoofbeats outside his office. He stepped out just as Tennant's riderless mount trotted up. The horse neighed and pawed the ground.

'Where's Grant?' he asked, as if the animal could understand and tell him his foreman's whereabouts.

Brad had underestimated the mount. Tennant's horse turned and went back along the road. Soon Connors found his foreman. What had happened? He saw that Tennant had been shot and was dead. Brad had heard no shot. Did Koesler do this? If so, he would have to prove it. But how? He had noticed earlier that Koesler was armed. Still, the

Gila foreman had come bearing well-wishes and offering Dunne's money. No, it couldn't have been Koesler.

Two hours later, Connors, taking a wagon, brought Grant Tennant to Doc Whitman's office in Apche Bend. Doc, he knew, would take care of everything.

'Don't rightly remember if Grant had a family,' Doc said.

'No, he didn't. He was alone in the world like me. No wife, no brothers or sisters or parents living far as I know.'

'We'll see that he gets a decent burial, Brad, and I'll ask Parson Ashe to say a few words, everything nice and proper.' Doc paused. 'What do you reckon you'll do now, Brad?'

'I rightly don't know.'

Turning, he left Doc's office and drove his wagon back to his digs.

As he approached his mine, shut down for the night, a blast at the entrance sent timbers flying in every direction. First Hawthorne, then McAdam, and now himself! He stood up in his wagon looking at the devastation.

What to do? He sighed and decided to accept Dunne's offer. He turned his wagon back in the direction of the Benson mine. He planned to tell McAdam of his decision and McAdam could tell the others in the MPA. What good was the MPA anyway?

What else was there for a man to do? Earlier, he had tried to hold his shoulders back in the presence of Koesler. Now, the world weighed heavily on him once more.

FOURTEEN

They buried Grant Tennant the next afternoon, a Tuesday. The day had been hotter than normal and sultry and the small band of friends and acquaintances who had gathered for the services stood bareheaded under a merciless sun.

Gabriel Ashe read the 23rd Psalm then launched into burial rites that he had put together from bits and pieces of scripture. When he came to the 'ashes to ashes, dust to dust' part, he stuttered over the words without intending to do so. Embarassed, the parson just stood there by the open grave, unable to continue.

Doc Whitman grinned and said: 'Gabe, we all knew Grant couldn't make it through a sentence without his tongue getting in the way. I figure right now he feels mighty comfortable with your sharing his stammering ways.'

Those gathered in the cemetery smiled. Matt Felkins said: 'Reckon Grant will stutter his way right through them Pearly Gates.'

Brad Connors limped over to Neil.

'I aim to take Caleb Dunne up on his offer.'

Parson Ashe, noting that Connors had left the grave site of his foreman waited patiently in the blistering sun.

'Brad, don't!' Neil pleaded.

'Ain't got much choice, Neil. I'm too old to stick it out. I needed Tennant, tongue-tied and all.'

'Can't you see that's what Dunne wants?'

'He's too powerful, Neil.'

'He hasn't paid the Olsens yet. Will you wait just a mite longer?'

Connors fixed his gaze on the wood coffin waiting to be lowered into Tennant's grave, but his words were directed to Neil.

'Reckon you've put up with more than the rest of us on behalf of Miss Benson, I'll wait a week but that's all.'

Connors limped back to the few people who had gathered for the services. Several men of Connors' crew who had worked under Grant Tennant's supervision slowly lowered the coffin into the grave. Connors threw a handful of dirt on to the wooden box.

Neil did the same. He shook his head. There had been violence and injuries at the mines, but Tom Benson and now Grant Tennant had paid with their lives.

How could Neil hold the mine owners together? How could he help bring an end to the threats against them all, and protect Merle from losing everything Tom Benson had left her? Would he survive another attempt on his life? Did someone really mean to kill him or simply scare him away from Apache Bend?

At the same time as Grant Tennant was laid to rest, a lone rider paused briefly at San Pablo, 35 miles south of Gila Crossing. He went into the general store, the San Pablo bank, and the Three Dog

Saloon which boasted that Bret Harte had proclaimed it the best watering hole to slake a man's thirst in Arizona Territory.

The rider carried a tintype of a slim youth of no more than 18, wearing a Confederate army uniform and a cap that barely concealed a mop of blond hair. He showed the picture to all the townspeople he could get to stop and look at it.

'Have you seen this man?' was the question he always asked. 'Name of Neil McAdam.'

He had grown accustomed to the shake of the head that invariably answered his query. He had come to expect the 'no' or the 'can't say I have, Mister' that was handed him after townspeople studied the tintype.

As he always did after a fruitless quest, the man rode off to the next town or crossing to the south and west. He knew that the people he stopped were seldom curious. The War Between the States was over and Union Blue or Rebel Gray was of small matter to them. He found, too, that wherever he went there was little love for a bounty hunter. Sometimes he felt he was close to his prey. At other times he sensed that the trail he followed was as cold as a snow-laden mountain top, a trail that led to nowhere. Could it be that Neil McAdam, if he were still alive, was beyond the law?

The lone rider would not give up. He spurred his horse on.

As with most towns in the Territory, it was the custom in Apache Bend that, following a funeral, those who had attended gathered at the home of the deceased's family for a meal contributed by women relatives and friends. Grant Tennant had no family. His home had been a one-room adobe hut a few yards from Brad Connors' house. Brad Connors, too, had no family, but he had many friends among the mine owners and their crews.

Millie Hawthorne, Rebecca Felkins, Dolly Meadows, Betsy Vanderman, Amy Gentian and Merle brought enough food to Connors' house to feed half of Apache Bend for a week. There were smoked hams, slow-cooked beans and molasses, pickled cucumbers, baked squash and steaming Indian pudding. Connors' rough-hewn dining room table was nearly covered with food and the dishes and utensils brought over by the ladies.

'Can't pull stakes now, Brad, until the grub's gone,' Neil said.

Brad nodded. 'I promised a week,' he told Lars Olsen. 'Maybe you and the missus will stick with me, eh?'

Lars cast an appealing glance at his wife. Ingrid Olsen frowned but said nothing.

'A week? I will do it I think, and then we must go,' Lars said.

No one at the after-funeral repast mentioned the fact that Caleb Dunne and his foreman, Dieter Koesler, or any of the Gila mine's crew, had appeared at Grant Tennant's burial or at Brad Connors' house afterwards.

After the meal, Neil rode Lady back to the Benson mine's office. Merle had stayed with the ladies to help put away things at Connors' place, and to make sure he had food to last him the week.

Neil wanted to go over the books and check the Benson output for the past seven days. Night had fallen when he finished. He extinguished the lamp and sat a few moments in the darkness. He lit one of Tom Benson's pipes and settled back to enjoy it. He wondered whether or not he had gained enough time to find out who was behind the mishaps that had plagued so many of the mine owners. And why. Brad Connors and Lars Olsen had promised to hold off Caleb Dunne for a week. Would a week be enough to find out the answers? Only Hawthorne and Felkins and Merle Benson remained to ward off the buy-outs that Dunne had offered. Neil knew he needed all the help he could get. He'd need even more some lucky break to unravel the tangle of mystery that had the mine owners in its grip.

He extinguished his pipe carefully. Then he lay back on the buffalo robes. The warmth of the mid-August night and the softness of the robes soon lulled him to sleep, a sleep that thrust him quickly once again into the nightmare that had haunted him for so many years.

1865! The surrender of the Confederate troops to William Tecumseh Sherman. Rebels handing over their rifles to the Union conquerors. Sad-eyed men, men and boys red-eyed from held-back tears. The stars and bars hauled down.

There was his brother, revenge-bent, raising his rifle and taking aim at Sherman. There was himself crying 'No! no!' and trying with his own rifle to knock Phil's weapon aside. Instead, with a deafening roar his rifle discharges. The bullet tears across his twin's forehead leaving blood in its wake. Phil slumps to the ground, mortally wounded. There is pandemonium.

As Cain did when he killed his brother Abel, Neil

in his nightmare bolts from the ranks and flees. The fires of remorse and guilt flee with him, consume him in their flames, suffocating him in their dense smoke.

Neil awoke, sweating, choking, eyes burning.

The office was ablaze.

Neil flung himself off his Indian bed and stumbled out of the building. A moment later, still dazed, he stood outside and watched the flames devour every timber, every wooden item, in the small structure. The adobe bricks blackened quickly from the heat and smoke.

His thoughts leaped to Lady tethered at the rear of the office. He sped to the lean-to. He whipped off his shirt and wrapped it over Lady's eyes, loosened her, then led the panic stricken palomino to safety.

Neil and his horse stood aside from the burned-out office. He watched the last of the flames die down. He looked at his pocket watch. It was four a.m. He knew he was lucky to be alive. McAdam surveyed the smoldering ashes of what had been his domain. The records, the books, the files, were beyond salvaging. Everything was destroyed.

Could he have started the fire? Had sparks from Tom Benson's pipe been the cause? No! Using a lantern that always hung in the nearby privy, he gingerly poked among the ruins while suffering the intense heat that still lingered. His boots and britches protected him but his bare torso, arms and hands soon reddened.

At one corner he found a gasoline can. So, he swore to himself, someone had doused the office and set it afire. Someone? Who? The gasoline can was blackened but he wiped the smudges of smoke from it by rubbing it against his britches. He read *Gila Mine* on the side of the can.

Caleb Dunne's mine. Damn it to hell, Dunne's Gila digs!

Was Dunne behind this? As strong as the evidence appeared to be, Neil could not believe Dunne would be, could be, so stupid. Was someone else trying to put the blame on Dunne? If so, who? Maybe it was the nephew of the mine owner, Joel Dunne, who was wanted for his father's murder. Neil dismissed the thought. Joel Dunne, if he was smart, would have put Arizona Territory far behind him. Joel was just a kid. How smart would he be?

Neil sat down beside Lady. Whoever was behind the attempts on his life was getting bolder. Whoever was behind it did not know the grit and determination that stiffened the backbone of Neil McAdam. Whoever was the mastermind did not know of the promises Neil had made at the grave site of Tom Benson, had made to Tom's daughter, and had made to himself. There was power in a promise and Neil would abide by that.

As he sat waiting for dawn that Wednesday morning, he remembered that he and his twin had been born on a Wednesday. Wednesday's children. What was that poem his mother used to read to him?

Wednesday's child is full of woe,
Thursday's child has far to go …

He could not remember the beginning of it or the end.

Woe had dogged the footsteps of the brothers,

that was certain. Phil was dead and Neil, having killed his twin, had been on the run for eight tormented years.

How could he ever be worthy of Merle Benson?

As dawn turned the mountain ridges crimson, somewhere south of the Gila, the lone horseman rode into still another town. He showed the tintype to everyone he met.

'Have you seen this man?'

The questions, the answers, were always the same wherever he rode – Kansas, Oklahoma, Texas, New Mexico. How many times had he heard good people say: 'Bounty hunter! That's a helluva way for a man to earn a living!' He rode on. If Neil McAdam was alive, there was no place he could hide.

FIFTEEN

When Zack Meadows, Ken Vanderman, and Neil's crew reported for work early on that Wednesday morning, they found Neil waiting for them at the Benson mine's entrance. They stared at the blackened ruins of the office.

Neil explained about the fire. He held up the gasoline can that he'd discovered. Zack noticed the Gila Mine identification on its side. He raised an eyebrow to ask a wordless question.

'Maybe Caleb Dunne, maybe not,' Neil said.

'You all right, boss?' Ken Vanderman asked.

'Maybe singed a bit from the heat, that's all.'

'I'll get a crew going on the office,' Zack promised. 'They're getting to be old hands at it. Probably take us a little longer than last time, but at least the adobe walls are still standing.'

This latest attack on the Benson digs and himself was sure to weaken Brad Connors' and Lars Olsen's resolve to stick it for another week before caving in to Dunne. He'd have to make his moves, whatever they might turn out to be, swiftly and quietly

An hour later, he finished reporting the latest set-back to Merle. Lady had been tethered alongside Firefly in Merle's stable, but Neil had not taken the time to rub her down.

'They'll stop at nothing!' Merle exclaimed. She stamped her foot to emphasize her exasperation.

'They? I don't think there are more that one who's behind it all Merle. Given a stroke of luck, and I'll need it, I'll find out who the sidewinder is.' He sat down at her kitchen table. 'I'll need help completing new records. Try to remember as much of our output as you can, our sales, our profits.'

'We'll manage, Neil. I've made notes on all your reports.'

He rubbed his eyes. 'I'm really tired, Merle. It's been a rough night. Can we work on the books tomorrow?' He turned to leave.

'Where are you going?'

'I figure I'd take a room at the Tumbleweed.'

'The Tumbleweed!' She stamped her foot again, this time to show her indignation. 'You'll do nothing of the sort, Neil. I won't hear of it. By rights now, my house will have to be our office until the one at the mine is rebuilt. Stay here. There's daddy's room, and you can take your meals here, too. I insist.'

He grinned and ran a hand through his sandy hair. 'You know how folks'd talk.'

She matched his grin with one of her own. 'Not if I charge you room and board, and I will. It's all honest and on the level.'

'Still, people gossip, Merle.'

'Neil, I didn't want to say this but I guess I have to. I want you to stay here because – because I'm frightened to be alone.'

Her admission disturbed him. 'Trouble follows me, Merle.' Oh, how he wanted to declare himself now, to do more that just court her, to ask her to marry him and set a date, but again he held back. 'There are things about me that you should know.'

'I know all I need to know. I'm scared to be alone. Will you – will you pay me room and board and stay?'

He sighed. 'I reckon I will. Can I lay down in Tom's room and get some sleep?'

She nodded. She took a kerosene lamp and led him into her father's bedroom. She turned down the patchwork quilt on the bed and fluffed the pillows.

'I'll undress now, Merle.' He waited for her to leave.

'Everyone knows daddy had his own private entrance. We know there's a door from the living room into here. *Our* private door.' She began to unbutton his shirt. Her fingers grew faster as she reached in to caress his chest. She stood on tiptoe to kiss his nipples. He stiffened.

He undressed her, she undressed him, and, naked, they slid into the bed that had been her father's. He felt at last, fully, that he had taken Tom Benson's place in Merle's life. He had gone beyond the protector that her father had been. He was both protector and lover.

They made love in the warmth of the room, so unlike the time before when rain pummelled their lean-to and they had shivered with cold and dampness as well as passion. She was his woman and he vowed to be all the man she would or could desire in her life. He would be her husband, unstraying, and would face whatever justice he was bound to meet. He was a fool to think he could escape his past.

Spent, he sighed and held her close. He covered her face with kisses. Then, though his ardor fought against it, the strain of the fire and all the events that had preceded it, the worry and the fight he knew he faced on behalf of the mine owners, was too much to rekindle passion. This time it was he who rolled over and fell asleep.

He awoke to the smell of coffee and sizzling pork chops and fried potatoes. He saw that Merle had filled the pitcher on Tom Benson's rough commode. She had also placed a large, thick towel on the rack alongside. Neil found Tom's straight razor, shaving mug and soap, and brush, shaved and washed himself, then combed his hair, which reeked of smoke.

Neil came into the kitchen and saw that Merle had already set a place for him. 'I was about to call you,' she said.

He finished the meal she had prepared, topping it off with a hug slab of apple pie and a second cup of coffee. Well fed, he pushed his chair away from the table.

'Everything I owned was destroyed by the fire. I'm going to ride into town and get some gear at the general store. Can I take the buckboard? I'll be back afore supper.'

'You don't need to ask, darling.'

He purchased pants, shirts, boots, a belt and underclothes from Frank Yegelstrom, and charged it to the mine's operating costs. Newly outfitted, and avoiding questions from townspeople, he headed back to the Benson house.

They spent the afternoon in attempting to

recreate the mine's records. Between them, they managed to approximate the figures that were destroyed in the fire.

'Close enough, I reckon,' Neil said. 'I'm just damned sorry all this has happened.'

'In one way I am, too. In another, I'm happy because it brought you closer to me.'

'There's one thing I'm bound to ask, Merle.'

'Yes?'

'It's been weeks since you promised. Will you play *Jeannie With the Light Brown Hair* for me, and sing it, too?'

'Of course I will.'

She sat down at the pianoforte in the parlor. He saw how the light of the kerosene lamp above the keyboard put golden glints in her brown curls.

Her voice was low as she sang and played the beloved Stephen Foster song. Just as she finished there came a knock at the front door. A timid knock at first, which changed quickly to a frantic pounding. Cautioning quiet with a finger to his lips, and wishing he had his .44, Neil went to the door and flung it open.

A young man stood on the porch. He was shaking and Neil sensed that it was because of fear as the night air was not chill. The man was thin almost to the point of emaciation. His clothes were ragged. He had not shaved for probably weeks. His eyes were lost in deep, dark hollows above his gaunt cheeks.

'Please, I've nowhere to go. I saw you and Miss Benson through the window. Will you hide me? I'm so hungry.' With those words he staggered and started to fall. Neil caught him and pulled him into the house.

Merle came from the parlor to see who had knocked. She stared at the young man. Her brown eyes widened at his wretched appearance.

'Who is it, Neil?'

'Joel Dunne. Quick! Close the curtains!' He led Joel to a chair. 'Did anyone see you come here?'

'I don't think so, Mr McAdam. I'm sure no one did.'

'I'll get coffee and a plate of food for him,' Merle said, and she hurried to the kitchen.

A few moments later, Merle came back with a mug of strong coffee and a ham sandwich. The boy was ravenous and twice Neil had to force him to slow down, to chew carefully, to pause between bites.

When Joel had finished eating, Neil spoke in reassuring tones. 'I want you to tell me where you've been, what you've been doing. And I want the truth, boy. Did you kill your father?'

'No, no,' he cried. 'I didn't kill my dad, so help me God!'

Then the youth told a story of greed and deceit and treachery so harrowing that Merle paled when she heard it. He could not hide any more, he stated. He had been hiding in one mine tunnel after another, but not in the Gila digs. He always managed to slip away in time, like an elusive shadow that disappears when the sun slips behind a cloud. He scavenged for food wherever he could find it. Often the food was spoiled or close to rotting and he grew sick. He counted on his Uncle Caleb, Sheriff Rengert, and other deputies figuring that he would put miles between him and Apache Bend.

'I saw the three men ride into town to start that

fight in the Sagebrush. My uncle hired them. He kept them hidden at the Gila mine. I watched them push that wagon into your office, but I slipped away before they saw me. I'm not sure, but I think it was Uncle Caleb's foreman who shot at you.'

'I can believe Dieter Koesler would do that.'

'I'm sure he shot Mr Tennant, too, but that I can't prove. I can't prove he dynamited your mine, Miss Benson, or Mr Connors' digs. I think he caused the cave-in at your mine, Miss Benson, 'cause I saw him do that at the Gila on the 4th of July.'

Merle offered Joel another cup of coffee as he continued his story.

'It's the coffee, I think, that did it,' the youth said.

'Did what?'

'The night my father was murdered, he and I went to see Uncle Caleb. Dad accused my uncle of cheating on the books. They owned the Gila together and dad wanted an accounting. He didn't trust Mr Koesler either. Dad took me along as a witness.

'Uncle Caleb said blood was thicker'n water and brothers should stand together. He figured my dad was mistaken. He sure tried to make us feel t'home. He gave dad and me some cake his housekeeper had made and some coffee. Like I said, I think the coffee did it. He must have drugged it with something, I don't know, and I don't remember finishing it.

'When I came to I was half-kneeling by my dad. There was a gun in my hand, my dad's gun. Dad was dead. Uncle Caleb said he saw me shoot his brother and that he'd see me hung. I didn't do it, I swear. I lit out.'

Joel began to tremble and Neil put an arm around his thin shoulders to comfort him.

'I was watching through the window at that mine owners' meeting. I saw how you stood up to my uncle, how you hit him and knocked him down. I knew then that you were the only one I could trust. I followed you and Miss Benson that night of the storm and I wanted to wake you but I didn't have the nerve.'

He gave a big sigh and slumped back in the chair.

'If you didn't kill your dad, Joel, then who did?'

'I'd say my uncle, or maybe Mr Koesler, but I can't prove it. The gun was in my hand. It was still smoking and Uncle Caleb swore he saw me do it. No one will believe me. He's important, respected. I'm nobody.'

'Maybe he's not as respected as you think, Joel. Do you know of any reason why your uncle would kill his own brother?'

'No.' Then Joel straightened. 'Yes. He always wanted to buy my dad out, but dad wouldn't sell. He said his share was my inheritance. Maybe Uncle Caleb did it to get my dad's and my share of the Gila.'

'And maybe you've hit the truth right on the button, Joel,' Neil said, 'right on the button. I think you sure as hell have.'

He saw that Joel hadn't heard him. The boy had put his head down on his folded arms at the table. He had fallen asleep. Neil raised Joel's head then he slipped one of the exhausted boy's arms around his shoulder. Neil lifted him and headed for the kitchen.

'Is he all right?' Merle's voice was tinged with anxiety.

'He's fine,' Neil assured her as he crossed the room. He sniffed. 'But the kid needs a bath. For sure he'd frighten a skunk. I'll ply him with coffee while you get the tub ready.'

SIXTEEN

While Merle filled the tin bathtub with hot water from the reservoir at the side of the stove, Neil made Joel stand. He forced the boy to drink more coffee. The runaway protested but Neil admonished him to stay awake long enough to get rid of the dirt.

'Get undressed!' Neil ordered. 'Don't be ashamed because Miss Benson's here.' He watched Merle test the water's temperature with her elbow. She looked up.

'That's how you do it for a baby's bath,' she explained.

'The kid ain't no baby, Merle. Please leave us.' Neil helped the boy undress, and when Merle left the kitchen, he picked up Joel again and plopped the naked kid in the tub.

Once Joel's face and body were covered with lather, Neil decided to shave the dark stubble that, at the boy's young age, already heralded the full beard he would shortly have to tackle.

Although he had never shaved any face other than his own, Neil did a creditable job. In five minutes, Joel's gaunt cheeks, upper lip and chin, were smooth as a young boy's.

Neil led Joel, who now had a dry towel around

him, into Tom Benson's bedroom. As they passed Merle, Neil smiled at the mine owner.

'If you don't pay no mind, Merle, I reckon Joel ought to sleep in a real bed for tonight. I'll stretch out on the settee in the parlor.'

Neil led young Joel into Tom's bedroom and put him into bed. 'Poor kid,' he muttered. 'This'll be the best sleep of your life.'

Neil blew out the kerosene lamp and moving with moccasin-like silence rejoined Merle in the parlor.

'I'll wash his clothes and iron his shirt tomorrow,' Merle promised.

'He's about my size – almost,' Neil said. 'I'll outfit him with some of my clothes, too. He can pay me when he's on his feet again, when he's got back his rightful share of the Gila digs.'

'If ever,' Merle said, sighing. 'Do you think Joel Dunne is telling the truth?'

Neil nodded. 'I do, I believe him. Running away like he did only made him look guilty. It doesn't mean he is.'

A troubled expression came over Neil's face as he spoke. He thought of his own flight and wanderings. Gosh, if only those had made him *look* guilty instead of being *branded* with good reason with the mark of Cain.

'I believe him,' Neil repeated. 'His story fits the things I've suspected all along about Caleb Dunne.'

'I thought he was a decent man,' she said. 'He offered to help me out.'

'*Buy* you out,' Neil emphasized.

'My daddy used to say that there's a little bit of bad in a good man and a lot of good in a bad man,' Merle said.

'Maybe that's why your father gave me a job,' Neil said, smiling.

'And maybe that's why I wanted you to be my manager. Oh, Neil, I could never believe anything bad about you.'

Neil's eyes misted at the trust she showed, the pure and simple goodness of this girl he loved. How could he ever tell her of his past?

'I want to marry you,' he whispered.

'You're telling me that,' she whispered back. 'What's keeping you from asking?'

'The trouble at the mines,' he said, knowing that was not the reason. 1865, General Sherman, the death by his hand of his twin brother, Phil: those were the real reasons.

The following morning, Neil was aroused by the mid-August sun. His back and legs were stiff from sleeping in a cramped position on Merle's velveteen settee.

He wandered into the kitchen and checked Merle's calendar. Thursday. Good. That meant there were three more productive days this week at the Benson mine. He hoped, too, that he could get to the bottom of the series of disastrous events at the Apache Bend silver mines before another mine owner sold out to Caleb Dunne.

Could he learn the truth? Could he do what needed to be done before Sunday? It would be good to have a Sunday during which nothing distressful happened. Merle would appreciate that. She ought to be up by now.

It was as if she divined his thought. Merle came into the kitchen, looking self-possessed and serene as if the startling drama of the night before had not affected her sleep one whit.

'Out of the kitchen, Neil!' she ordered. ''Tis a woman's domain. I'll have breakfast ready in two shakes.' She glanced at the small locket watch she wore on a blue ribbon around her slim neck. 'Gracious, it's really time for the noon meal. See if Joel has rested enough to come to the table in about a half hour.'

Neil grinned. What a woman. She could rustle up a meal in half an hour, no doubt of that. He headed for Tom's bedroom to wake up Joel, but he saw that there was no need to be the cock's crow. Joel was sitting on the edge of the bed.

'Where are my clothes, Mr McAdam?' he asked.

'Miss Benson aims to wash 'em. It'll take some doing before she can scrub the grime out.' He tossed one of his shirts to the youth. 'This oughtta fit you.'

As the youth dressed, Neil believed that the fugitive had gained some color in his face. Sunlight, good food and freedom from fear would do wonders for the son of the late Howard Dunne.

'You'll get a hearty dinner from Miss Benson, so come along.'

The noon meal was as substantial as Neil had promised. There were fried potatoes, crisp around the edges, thick slices of fatback, pole beans from Merle's garden at the rear of the adobe house, slabs of home made bread, newly-churned butter, strong coffee, wedges of chocolate-frosted cake.

Bowing his head, Neil asked that the food be blessed.

Upon Neil's "amen", Joel looked at the table, the plates, cups and utensils, the platters and bowls of food. Neil saw that the youth's eyes had misted, but that Joel was trying manfully to hold back tears.

Merle had noticed, too. 'You go right ahead and cry if you've a mind to. You've a right after what you've been through.'

'No ma'am, I'm not gonna cry. My dad wouldn't cotton to that if he could see me.' Joel managed a small grin. 'Besides, I'm too hungry to waste time on anything other than eating.'

When dinner was over, Neil pushed back his chair and stood.

'This part ain't gonna be easy, Joel, but it's something you gotta do.'

'What?'

'Go see Sheriff Rengert and tell him what you told us.'

'Mr McAdam, he'd never believe me. I should've lit outta the territory.'

'No, you did right coming to Miss Benson's house. Don't you worry, Joel. I'll go to the sheriff's office with you. Look, I'll stick by you every minute.'

'They'll hang me.'

'They'll have to string me up alongside, too, and they're not about to do that.' He turned to Merle. 'Can Joel ride Firefly?'

'Of course.'

A few moments later, Neil on Lady and Joel on Merle's horse, headed for Apache Bend. The weather was not promising. Dark clouds hung low over the road yet there was no feel of rain in the air. Neil had hoped for sun to help put a tan back in Joel's cheeks but he saw that his hope had failed him. Normally not superstitious, Neil nevertheless hoped that the ominous clouds were not an unwelcome omen.

Merle washed young Joel's clothes twice and hung
them out to dry. It was quite late in the day when
she decided to see the damage to the mine's office.
Perhaps the fire was greater than Neil had let on.
Perhaps he was trying to spare her feelings. Well,
Zack Meadows would tell her, that is if he and the
crew were still at work. If she rode fast enough
she'd reach the mine before Zack and the miners
shut down the shift for the day.

Joel had left on Firefly, so she had to saddle one
of the bays that she used to pull the buckboard.
Which one? Alden or Standish? Standish was
slower but steadier when saddled with a rider. She
chose Standish. The bay took off in high spirits.

The clouds drew darker as she rode on.

When she came to the mine she saw that the shift
had gone home. Everything appeared in good
order at the mine's entrance. She had no desire to
venture inside the tunnel. Dismounting, she poked
among the ashes of the office. She didn't notice the
gasoline can that Neil had told her about. How
could anyone do such a thing? How could anyone
cause a mine cave-in or dynamite one's digs? Was
Caleb Dunne the evil man that his nephew, Joel,
claimed him to be? Heartsick, she remounted the
bay.

Standish reared suddenly and Merle had all she
could do to keep the horse from bolting.

A man on horseback had appeared from
nowhere, or so it seemed to her. He dismounted
and walked slowly toward the mine entrance. Then
Standish whinnied. Startled, the man stopped.
Merle, keeping a tight rein on her bay to steady

him, approached the stranger. At close range, she saw he wasn't a stranger, but Dieter Koesler. He held a tightly-tied package in one hand an a length of fuse in the other. He set the package down at his feet.

'What are you doing here, Mr Koesler?' She dismounted and picked up the package. Recognizing at once the sticks of dynamite, Merle looked up and saw Koesler, who, as he backed away, took a gun from his holster. His face was a mask of fear and hatred.

'You see too much, lady,' he said. 'This cannot happen.' His accent had thickened and Merle could barely hear him.

'You were going to dynamite the mine, weren't you? Is that what Mr Dunne ordered? That's how my father was killed. That's how Neil McAdam was almost killed. Now, a third time?' Her eyes blazed with anger. 'Sheriff Rengert will hear about this.'

'Mr Dunne has the sheriff in his hands. You see too much, lady,' he repeated. 'I apologize to you.'

With those words, Koesler fired.

Merle gave a cry of anguish as the bullet struck home. She felt a sharp stab of pain in her left arm and watched the blood stain widen on her sleeve. She knew she must not let Koesler fire again. She must let him think he had mortally wounded her. She lay inert beside the restless front legs of Standish. She looked up and whispered to the frightened horse, 'Go home, boy, go home.'

Free of restraint the bay galloped off. Merle saw him head down the direction from which he had come, back to the Benson house and stable.

Merle, possum-like, remained as still as if death had claimed her. She was aware of Koesler walking over to her. She heard him grunt, then pick up the sticks of dynamite. Would he now blow up the mine? She heard him walk away. She thought, he's satisfied I'm dead. She opened her eyes. What was he doing? She saw him mount his horse. Perhaps fear of discovery had changed his course. He rode off in a direction that would take him, she knew, in a wide arc around Apache Bend.

She sat up and examined her wound. The bullet had only grazed her arm, a flesh-wound her dad would have labelled it, but it was painful, it bled, and it hurt a lot. She tore a narrow strip from her petticoat and wrapped it around the wound. She was certain that she was in no danger of bleeding to death. Someone would come along and find her. She regretted now that she had urged Standish to leave. At the same time, she was proud of the way she had fooled Koesler.

The bleeding had stopped, but the pain in her arm, throbbing as if a rattlesnake had struck it, did not cease. Her feint had deceived Koesler, but now it became a real faint.

She blacked out.

At the same time Merle had left her house on the saddled Standish, Neil and Joel rode into Apache Bend. They faced the stares of townsfolk on the board sidewalks.

'That's him, the kid who murdered his daddy,' one man cried out. 'Recognized him from the posters.'

'Yes,' said a woman loud enough to be heard across the street, 'that's Howard Dunne's boy. Caught him at last!'

'Hangin's not good enough for a whelp who'd

kill his own daddy,' said the man who had first spotted the two riders.

'What's the kid doing with the manager of Miss Benson's mine?' another nosy man asked. 'Neil McAdam sure ain't no deppity.'

'Pay them no mind, Joel,' Neil said. 'They're just looking for a scapegoat. They'll be surprised when they learn the truth.'

Neil and Joel dismounted and tied their horses to the hitching rail in front of the sheriff's office. Neil saw that the youth's hands shook as he looped the reins of Firefly around the rail.

'You've tethered Firefly too tight, Joel, give the horse some slack.' He grinned, hoping that would give the young man some assurance. 'And allow yourself some slack, too.'

He wanted to make sure Joel did not feel lonely and without a friend.

'All right,' Neil said, 'let's *both* go in and face the music.'

SEVENTEEN

If Neil thought the townspeople would be surprised at the sight of Howard Dunne's boy, he saw that no one could be more astonished than Sheriff Guy Rengert when Neil brought Joel into Rengert's office and town lock-up.

'Well, I'll be damned!' Rengert exclaimed. 'Wait'll Caleb Dunne hears of this. He's been after me for weeks to bring the kid in.'

'You just stay in that chair, Sheriff,' Neil said, 'and hold your tongue until Joel here tells his story.'

Rengert, as usual, did as he was told. He listened to everything the youth had to say. At times, Rengert's eyes showed disbelief. At other times they indicated a begrudging sympathy.

It took Joel an hour to relate his story.

'Then I came to Miss Benson's house and told them what I just told you, sir. Mr McAdam and Miss Benson took me in.'

'Maybe they got blinders on,' Rengert said. 'You tell a good fairy tale kid, oughtta start with once upon a time. Still, I gotta arrest you.'

'Fair enough for now,' Neil said. 'For his own safety, keep him behind bars and outta sight. Sheriff, we had a fire last night at the Benson office. Turned the place into a barbecue pit.'

'That gal's sure been spooked, McAdam,' Rengert said.

'You're right, but by human spooks. I want you to come with me.'

Reluctantly, Rengert locked Joel in the small cell behind the sheriff's office. A few moments later he mounted his own horse and rode alongside Neil on Lady as they headed out of town. Neil held the reins of the riderless Firefly.

They made a brief stop at the Benson mine office.

'That's the gasoline can, Sheriff.'

'Don't prove Dunne set the fire, McAdam.'

'If it wasn't Dunne,' Neil argued, 'it could have been his head man, Koesler.'

'Seems odd it was left lying around here in what's left of your office.'

'You saying I planted it?' Neil questioned, his voice hot with anger. 'If you're thinking I did this, Sheriff, come along with me to Miss Benson's house. She heard Joel's story and can back him up.'

'Listen, McAdam, everyone in town knows she'll echo whatever danged thing you say.'

Neil thought he heard someone moan but he dismissed the sound as coming from the wind as it blew across the tunnel entrance. He noticed the sound caught Rengert's attention, too. The moan Neil heard was followed by a call for help.

'You hear that?' Neil asked.

'Probably a coyote howling off afar,' Rengert said.

'Coyotes can't speak. Come on! Sounds like it came from the mine.'

Still on foot, they raced to the mine's entrance.

They found Merle still lying down in the sand. She had been barely visible in the fading light of a cloud-darkened sky.

Neil took the prostrate girl in his arms. 'Merle, Merle,' he whispered, 'what are you doing here? You're bleeding.'

'I was shot, Neil, but I don't think it's serious. My arm, yes, it bled some. I think I fainted.'

'Who shot you, Miss Benson?' Rengert demanded.

'It was Mr Dunne's foreman, Sheriff. I caught him just as he was getting set to dynamite my mine – again.'

Neil turned to the sheriff. 'Now do you believe who's behind all this? Now do you see what kind of varmint Caleb Dunne is?'

Rengert pursed his lips. 'You think Dunne gave orders to Koesler to do this?'

'Sure as there's silver in this mine, Sheriff,' Neil said.

'One thing, Sheriff,' Merle said, 'Koesler said that Mr Dunne had you in his hands.'

'In his hands, eh? Well, we'll see about that.'

For the first time, since he had known the sheriff, Neil saw a resolute look on Rengert's face.

'I've got Firefly here,' Neil said to Merle. 'Can you ride back to your house okay?' He helped her mount her horse.

'Sure I can. I'll be all right, Neil.'

'I'll send Doc Whitman around just to make sure.'

Neil put his boot into the stirrup and swung up onto Lady's saddle. He brought the horse alongside Firefly. He leaned over toward Merle and, unmindful of the sheriff, kissed her. 'Hang on to the reins tightly,' he said, 'but only with your right hand.' She was pale because of her ordeal, but to Neil her pretty face was more beautiful than ever.

'Darling, darling,' he murmured. Then he found the courage to ask the question he had for so long kept from asking.

'Merle, will you marry me?'

'Yes, oh yes,' she whispered.

Sheriff Rengert shook his head. 'I ain't sure I'm hearing right, you two. McAdam, this ain't no time to propose to a gal.'

Merle managed a smile. 'Sheriff, every woman knows that any time's a good time.'

Neil and Rengert dug spurs into their horses' flanks. In less than half an hour they reached Doc Whitman's house at the edge of town. They found Doc seated in a rocker on his porch.

'Doc, Merle's been shot by Koesler. She's all right. She's at her house, but she's bled more'n a mite. Will you go there and see that she's okay?'

Doc Whitman nodded. 'I'm right off, Neil. Where you going?'

'We're after Caleb Dunne.'

'Well, you ain't got far to go,' Doc said. 'He's at the Sagebrush Saloon right now. Been there a spell in a poker game.' I heard he's winning handsome at five card stud.'

'Maybe his luck's run out,' Rengert said.

'Soon's I saddle old Alamo, I'm on my way, Neil.' Then Doc grinned at Rengert. 'Sure good to see you riding in the right company, Sheriff. Makes that there tin star shine a little brighter.'

* * *

Neil and Rengert rode on until they came to Rengert's office and the lockup.

'I aim to make this a face to face deal,' Rengert said. 'I aim to take Joel with us just 'cause Dunne's been hounding me to bring the kid in.'

Neil and the sheriff tethered their mounts to the porch rail of the sheriff's office. then Neil, Rengert and Joel walked across the street to the Sagebrush. Dunne's chestnut horse was prominent among several mounts tethered at the hitching rail.

'I recognize Ginger, too,' Neil said.

'Ginger? Whose horse might that be?' the sheriff asked.

'Brad Connors' mount.'

As if mention of Connors' name was a summons, the mine owner limped through the swinging half-doors on to the board sidewalk.

He looked startled as he spied Joel Dunne but relaxed as if the sight of Joel in the custody of the sheriff assured him that law if not order prevailed in Apache Bend.

'Dunne's inside, Brad?' Neil questioned.

'Table at the rear with a couple of cronies. Winning big.'

'We're after Dunne,' Neil explained. 'We're going in slow and easy. Koesler shot Miss Benson, she's okay, but I'm sure Dunne put him up to it.'

Brad whistled softly at that news.

'Brad, will you round up the others, Hawthorne and Felkins and Olsen, and get back here? If we're not at the Sagebrush head for Dunne's mine.'

'Fast as you can, Connors,' Rengert urged. 'There's gonna be a showdown either here or there.'

Connors mounted his roan and galloped off.

The two men and the youth went into the saloon. A number of the patrons, mostly mine workers, moved out of the way as they spotted the sheriff. Their glances at Joel, Neil felt, were more curious than hostile.

The sheriff and Neil had guns, Joel was unarmed. As they moved with deliberate slowness toward the rear of the room near the bar where, Neil remembered, three thugs had put Zack and Ken out of commission.

Dunne's back was to them. When others at the table glanced at the advancing three, Dunne turned. He rose.

'I knew you'd do your duty, sooner or later, Sheriff,' Dunne said. 'I wanted nothing more than to see you bring Joel, this murdering pup, in.'

'I didn't kill nobody and you know it, Uncle Caleb,' Joel said.

'Kid, you ain't the man your daddy was.' Dunne faced the miners in the room. 'Wasn't anybody more of a square shooter than my brother, Howard. You folks know that. I grieve for what my nephew did.' He turned back to face Joel. 'Sorry to see this happen to kin, but the sheriff's ready to see you hanged.'

'I ain't seeing to nothing of the sort, Dunne,' Rengert said.

'What d'you mean?' Dunne's dark eyes blazed with anger as he questioned Rengert. 'You collared him, didn't you? Arrested him like I told you to?'

Rengert took a step closer to Dunne. 'I don't do what you *tell* me, Dunne. Might do something if you *asked* me. Telling and asking are two different things.'

'Aw, you know what I mean, Guy.' Dunne's voice was placating.

'It's Sheriff, Dunne, not Guy.'

'You killed my dad, Uncle Caleb. It had to be you. No one else was there at your place 'cepting you, dad and me. You drugged my coffee, maybe my dad's, too.'

'Sheriff Rengert, are you going to listen to the kid's blather? Lock him up.'

Now, Neil took a step closer to Dunne. 'Where's Koesler?'

'I don't know. I don't keep track of him when he's off duty.'

'I don't know where he is now, either,' Neil said, 'but I know where he *was* not too long ago. He shot Miss Benson when she caught him at her digs.'

Suddenly Dunne's face paled. 'Koesler didn't shoot anybody. That's not what I told him to do.' Dunne grew even paler as he realized he had said too much. 'I mean I gave Koesler orders to drop around to see Miss Benson and offer my sympathies about the fire at her office.'

Neil put his hand to his holster but, as Rengert cautioned, he didn't draw. 'You gave Koesler orders to dynamite Miss Benson's digs. Right? When he was caught, Koesler shot.'

'Sheriff, are you going to listen to McAdam's ravings?'

'Reckon that's just what I'm doing,' Rengert replied. 'Miss Benson can identify Koesler.'

Dunne backed away slowly. 'Are you charging *me* with anything, Sheriff? Are you arresting me?'

'Did you kill my father, Uncle Caleb?' Joel questioned.

'Don't be stupid like your daddy, kid,' Dunne

said, backing still further from them. Gone was his grief for his brother. Square-shooter had become stupid.

With a sudden rapid movement, Dunne hurled a chair at Neil and the sheriff. He tipped over the table, and the cards and his winnings rolled all over the floor. There was a quick scramble by Dunne's cronies and a few miners to retrieve the money. In the excitement, Dunne bolted for the door.

Rengert drew and took aim at the fleeing mine owner, but Joel cried out at the sheriff. 'Don't shoot! He's blood kin!'

Neil heard the rapid hoofbeats of Dunne's chestnut stallion, first loud, then fading, as Dunne made his escape.

'Kid, you just obstructed justice,' Rengert said.

'Shooting Dunne isn't justice,' Neil said. 'Bringing him to trial is. I guess his actions sure clear Joel's name.'

'Well, then, let's go after him! Wasting any more time, Dunne'll be clean off to the hills.'

'No, he won't,' Joel said. 'He'll go straight to the Gila. Uncle Caleb only left the mine when he had to do business, go to a meeting, go to the stamping mill or pay a call on the bank.'

'Or play poker at the Sagebrush,' Rengert said, dryly.

'Anything else he'd leave to Mr Koesler. The Gila and silver were the most important things in the world to Uncle Caleb.'

'We've got fifteen miles of hard riding to do to get to the Gila digs,' Neil said. 'Let's get moving! Brad Connors and the rest can catch up with us there.'

They left the saloon and mounted their horses.

'Joel,' Neil said, 'hop up behind me on Lady, and hang on!'

The sheriff, Neil and Joel galloped off, the youth with his arms around Neil's waist. What if Joel was wrong, and his uncle hadn't returned to the Gila? The sky grew ever darker with black clouds. Now and then flashes of lightning lit up the fringes of the clouds. The feeling in the air reminded Neil of the time he and Merle had ridden out into the high desert, only now there was no sign of rain. Joel's tightening grip was an extra reminder that it had been the kid who stood by them, then vanished, while Merle and he slept in the crude lean-to.

Over and over two questions chased each other through Neil's mind: would Dunne reach the Gila and then hide out somewhere in the labyrinth of his mine? Would they be able to find him and bring him to justice before a jury of his peers?

Neil was afraid that the answer to the first question was *yes*, and the answer to the second was probably *no*.

EIGHTEEN

Caleb Dunne, riding hard on his stallion, carried nothing in his saddlebags but regrets. At a moment in which he felt trapped in the Sagebrush Saloon, recklessness had taken over his usual level-headed view of things. The presence of his nephew Joel had unnerved him. Worse, that lily-livered sheriff didn't appear to have the boy in custody. It was more like the kid had ceased to be a fugitive wanted for murder and had become the sheriff's deputy instead.

He'd gotten away from the Sagebrush easy enough, almost too easy, but he had no illusions that he was free from danger. He knew Rengert and McAdam and his nephew would lose little time in coming after him. Ah, but would they know where he was heading? He no sooner posed the question to himself than he realized that of course they would. Perhaps he could outfox them.

He'd lay low for as long as he wanted. Unknown even to Koesler and the Gila's crew, unknown even to his late brother, Howard, and Howard's boy, Joel, Dunne had, some months earlier, prepared a secret hideout in a lower tunnel. The tunnel had been mined out and was argentite dead. He had stored food and lanterns and matches there, as well as a cache of arms and ammunition.

Who knew, he reasoned, if his plans to acquire the other five silver mines that formed a parenthesis alongside Apache Bend would meet with passive resistance or open warfare between the other owners and himself? Were it to be warfare he wanted a secret bunker where he could retreat and hole up if necessary.

As Dunne galloped on to the Gila, Dieter Koesler and Frau Koesler, who serveyed as cook for Caleb Dunne, were packing the saddle bags on two horses with as many things as they could stuff into them. Clothes, beef jerky, corn meal, coffee, and pinto beans.

'The thing what is wrong now?' Frau Koesler asked.

'No time, woman, to tell you. Leaving must be done now, hurry. We will ride to the east far as we can.'

'You know I have not rode the horse for two years now.'

Koesler surveyed his wife's ample figure, gained from tasting too much of what she cooked. Tonight, Thursday, it would be *tapfelspitz* and freshly-ground horseradish, and tonight it would have to remain uneaten. 'You have padding enough to be easy on the horse,' he said. 'Hurry! Hurry!'

He helped his heavy wife on to the saddle of one of the Dunne's geldings, then he mounted his own horse. With Frau Koesler demanding an explanation and getting none, and with Koesler looking like a hunted animal, the two galloped away from the Gila digs.

* * *

A half hour later, Dunne rode up to the Gila's entrance.

His well-appointed office was dark. No light shone from his nearby house. Normally at this time in mid-August, there would be plenty of summer daylight. But with a storm gathering and with lowering clouds, someone had been wise enough to hang a lighted lantern above the mine's entrance.

He picked up a board and struck his chestnut mount across the flanks several times. The stallion whinnied and snorted and reared several times and then took off.

'Good! Keep going,' Dunne said to himself. 'They'll look for hoofprints and follow you. They'll think I'm still on you.'

He grabbed the lantern that hung over the mine's entrance and then ran into the main tunnel. After fifty yards the tunnel branched out into two lesser tunnels each of which were a hundred feet long. The configuration was that of a sprawling letter *Y*. The main tunnel, the *Y*'s stem, had four deep shafts sunk along its length. The arms of the *Y* had two deep shafts each.

As he raced along the ore cars' tracks in the main tunnel, a gust of wind blew out his lantern. He felt in his pocket for a match and he relit the lantern. Once again, a draft of wind blew out the lantern. He dug in his pocket for a handful of matches. In relighting the lantern, he dropped the remaining matches. Well, he'd retrieve them in a moment, but before he could do so, he stumbled and fell. The lantern broke on a rock and flamed out.

Moving more cautiously now he hugged the side

of the tunnel. Caution failed him. He bumped into an unfamiliar wooden barricade. It gave way with a sharp crack of dry lumber, and he plunged 30 feet to the first level of one of the shafts.

Shock waves from his broken ankles ran through his entire body. Now he remembered where he was and why. He was in the second from the last shaft in the main tunnel. This was the shaft in which Koesler had arranged the cave-in to fool the other miners the night of the box social on the 4th of July. Remembrance led to terror that took over his mind and body. He suddenly realized why the shaft opening was barricaded. His crew had quit working there because they ran into a nest of vinegaroons.

Dunne had landed in that nest of large whip scorpions believed by many in the high desert of Arizona Territory to be extremely venomous. When alarmed, as they now were, they emitted the vinegar odor that gave them their name.

Despite the shooting pains in his broken ankles, he felt the scorpions' vicious stings as they struck him above the top of his boots.

He screamed and screamed.

Rengert, Neil and Joel rode up to the Gila digs. From the mine entrance came the distant, hollow sound of screams. Whose? the three, as one, dismounted.

'Good Lord!' Rengert cried. 'What's that? What's happened to Dunne?'

'*If* that's Dunne we're hearing,' Neil said. He wasn't at all sure, because the screams ceased suddenly.

'We'll soon find out,' the sheriff said.

'What about Koesler?' Neil asked.

Joel glanced around the area. 'I don't see his horse,' he said, 'and there usually was another one tethered at that lean-to behind the office.'

'We'll need lanterns,' Rengert declared.

Joel sped to Dunne's house. A few minutes later he returned with three lanterns. 'Nobody t'home,' he said. 'There's a fire in the kitchen stove and food cooking, but nobody's there.'

'They lit out,' Neil said, anger edging his voice.

'Never mind Koesler and his woman,' Rengert said. 'No time for him now. He's good as dead. With no protection from Dunne he ain't got a chance. We'll get him sooner or later.'

The three headed for the mine's entrance and as they did so Connors, Hawthorne, Felkins and Olsen rode up.

'Follow us!' the sheriff commanded. 'Dunne's in there someplace.' With Rengert in the lead, holding his lantern high, the six other men were hard on his heels as they raced in the direction of the screams. Several times wind-drafts blew out their lanterns but the men quickly relit them.

Neil was the first to spot the broken barricade. The screams now were fainter. Neil peered down and, in the dim light of the lantern held by Connors, he saw the upturned face of Dunne. Faint as the lantern's glow was, Neil could make out the Gila owner's once dark features were now pallid with terror.

'Help me!' Dunne's agonized cry was desperate. 'You can't be so cruel as to leave me here!'

'Let's hear you admit a few things that you've done afore we help you,' Rengert called down.

'Yes, yes, anything Guy.'

'Did you arrange that cave-in at the Benson mine where Tom Benson was crushed to death?' Neil asked.

'Yes, yes. Get me out of here, I'm poisoned.'

'How about the dynamite explosion at my digs?' Hawthorne asked.

'And at Miss Benson's?' Neil put in, and then continued, 'How about the fight at the Sagebrush that messed up my foreman, Zack Meadows, and one of my crew, Ken Vanderman?' Neil turned to the others. 'Reckon I got more questions than anybody.' He leaned over the shaft. 'Who's responsible for trying to shoot me? For wrecking the Benson office one night and setting it afire another? Who moved and despoiled Tom Benson's grave marker? Who killed my horse Dixie?'

Brad Connors added his question and his anger along with Neil's. 'Who's responsible for killing my foreman, Grant Tennant?'

To all those questions, Dunne either responded with 'I'm at fault,' or 'Koesler did what I told him to do.' During the questioning, Dunne screamed again and pleaded 'Please help me!'

'One more question,' Sheriff Rengert said. 'Did you kill your brother, try to blame your nephew Joel, and steal Joel's rightful share of the Gila?'

'Yes! As God will judge me, yes.'

'You men heard him,' Rengert said to the others. 'A full confession. You're witnesses and you're gonna testify in a court of law. We'll judge him here in Apache Bend before God gets his licks in.'

Hawthorne grabbed a rope from a nearby ore car, made a lasso out of it, and lowered it to Dunne. The Gila owner put it around his waist. Felkins, Hawthorne, O'Neil and Olsen took hold of the rope and with little effort pulled the treacherous Dunne to the surface of the main tunnel.

During the time it took to do so, Caleb Dunne died.

'Caleb Dunne died from the stings of a score of vinegaroons,' Hawthorne said, his words solemn and measured.

'Not really,' Neil said, 'if you've no mind my saying so. Vinegaroons are not as venomous as most people think. Doc Whitman set me straight on that once.'

'Then what did this miserable skunk die from?' Connors asked.

Felkins looked down on Dunne's corpse. 'He died of fright, simple as that. I seen it afore, fighting Indians. Caleb Dunne was just scared to death. I'll put money on it.'

Hawthorne and Felkins carried Dunne down the length of the tunnel to the mine's entrance. The rest of the avenging party followed. Once outdoors, they found that night had fallen and that the storm clouds had drifted to the east. There was no lightning or rain. A nearly full moon had shoved aside the clouds that had hidden it and bathed the area in a pale light.

After Doc Whitman looked Dunne over, Sheriff Rengert said, 'Gabe Ashe has gotta give this varmint some kind of decent burial. Don't know that he deserves it, but the parson's the last word on it.'

Neil nodded. What had Merle said to him? Her father's words? *There's a little bit of bad in a good man and a lot of good in a bad man.* Yes, Caleb Dunne deserved a decent burial. There was good in all these men around him.

'Well, Brad,' Hawthorne said to Connors. 'I guess you got revenge for your foreman's murder. And, Lars,' he added, ''pears like you won't have to sell your digs after all. You and the missus can raise your little one right in Apache Bend, no finer place.'

'Nice sentiments, gentleman.' A voice came from the dim shadows of Dunne's house. 'I'm short on time. Which one of you scoundrels is Neil McAdam?'

Neil whirled, wary, defensive, and faced the shadows.

'I am,' he stated, then regretted it the moment he said it.

He reached for the .44 in his holster.

'Hold your fire, Neil. Why do you keep trying to shoot me? Especially since your aim ain't even Kentucky windage.' Phil McAdam stepped out of the shadows and revealed himself in the moonlight. He bore a scar from his hairline to his right brow.

Neil was stunned, but not too dazed to join his brother in a rebel yell that shattered the night. Phil came forth in the moonlight. In a moment, Neil and his brother were in each other's arms, locked in an embrace so tight that it appeared that the two men were one. Neil sobbed unashamedly. 'Phil, you're alive, alive!' he said over and over.

Hawthorne scratched his head and ran his hand through his dark hair. Felkins pulled on his sandy mustache. They both turned to Connors and Olsen.

'I don't know what the devil that's all about,' Hawthorne said, 'but I'll be blistered, Neil McAdam's got hisself a twin!'

NINETEEN

The sheriff, Joel and the four mine owners gaped with astonishment at the two look-alikes. Other than the clothes they wore, the McAdam brothers were identical, each a lean six feet in height, each with the same sandy hair and deep blue eyes.

'I guess I stumbled into some messy business.' Phil pointed to the dead Caleb Dunne.

Neil introduced his brother to the others, then gave a quick explanation as to why they were here and why Dunne was dead.

Sheriff Rengert carried Dunne in front of him on his horse. Phil McAdam, who had his own horse, joined Neil, Joel and the mine owners, and the little party headed back for Apache Bend.

It was close to midnight, only a few minutes before Thursday.

One by one the owners who had accompanied Rengert, Neil, Phil and Joel, dropped off at their places, first Hawthorne, then Olsen, then the sheriff at his office and lock-up, then Connors and finally Felkins.

To Neil's surprise, he and Joel found Rebecca Felkins and Millie Hawthorne taking care of Merle under Doc Whitman's watchful eye.

Neil introduced his brother to Doc, Merle and the ladies. Doc and Merle's gaze shifted from one to the other then back again, as did Rebecca's and Millie's.

'It's no mirage, folks,' Neil assured them. 'It's a long story but it can wait until later.' Merle was seated in a comfortable chair and Doc had put her bandaged arm into a sling. 'I'll be as good as new before you know it,' she said.

'This is the girl I'm going to marry,' he told Phil proudly.

Neil noticed the appreciative look in his brother's eyes as he smiled at Merle. It simply proved a fact that Neil had almost forgotten. His great-grandfather, his grandfather, his father – in fact all McAdam men, knew beauty when they saw it. Many a mint julep on Georgia verandahs had been raised in a toast to beauty.

Doc Whitman, when told that Caleb Dunne was dead, declared he'd pick up the body from Sheriff Rengert. When Doc departed, he took Joel along with him. 'I want to give you a thorough look-see,' he told the boy, 'and make sure your weeks in hiding didn't harm you too much.'

'We've fixed some vittles in the kitchen,' Rebecca Hawthorne said, ' 'cause we knew you'd be hungry. Ingrid Olsen would've joined us, but you know – what with a baby coming and all.'

Neil, helping Merle, repaired to the kitchen and Phil followed. As they partook of the food the ladies had prepared, Merle whispered to the two men. 'People are so good,' she said.

It wasn't until nearly dawn on Friday that the trio retired. It was agreed that, for the time being, Phil would bunk in with Neil in Tom's bedroom. The past 18 hours had been exhausting and the three slept until well past noon.

While they slumbered that Friday morning, Sheriff Rengert assured Joel that proper steps would be taken at once to restore the youth's rightful place in Apache Bend. Necessary papers would be prepared and signed by the local judge to guarantee that the Gila mine was Joel's and Joel's alone.

That Friday afternoon, while Merle and the twins were just awakening, Caleb Dunne was buried. He lay in a far corner of the little cemetery. Parson Ashe committed the mine owner to the judgment that all must face, saint and sinner alike.

Only Ashe, Doc Whitman and Joel Dunne were present.

'I'll see that Uncle Caleb gets a decent marker for his grave,' Joel said. 'I'll ask Mr Breihalter to fix up something.'

The parson remarked that Dunne should have an epitaph that lauded his virtues and not his vices.

Doc Whitman snorted. 'Won't need much space on the marker for that.'

It was not until the day following Dunne's burial, Saturday, that Neil felt up to telling his story. He was grateful that his brother did not press him, nor did Merle.

'Whenever you're ready, we'll talk,' Phil said.

So, after breakfast and with plenty of coffee to replenish their empty cups, Neil and Phil busied themselves in relating the events that changed their lives since '65 and the surrender of Confederate troops to General Sherman. Merle listened attentively to what each brother had to tell.

'When Neil tried to stop me shooting the general,' Phil told Merle, 'his rifle went off. The bullet ploughed this damn furrow in my forehead, knocked me flat off my feet. I blacked out, dead to the world. Guess I messed the place up with a lot of blood.'

'Dead to me, too, Phil. I was sure I killed you,' Neil said. 'In the excitement, with our men surrendering and all, I just lit out. I didn't know if they'd shoot me, and I'd sooner a Union shot would stop me so you and I would've died together. But I got away.'

'So I found out later,' Phil said. 'I figured you thought you killed me and it must hurt to think you were carrying that on your back.'

'What happened to you after that?' Neil asked.

'The Union army handed me a year in prison up north in Pennsylvania. Just a year 'cause Sherman wasn't touched. But the war was over and I guess they felt why should they spend Yankee dollars to put food in my belly and keep a roof over my head? So they let me go in three months.'

'Oh, Neil,' Merle said, 'that's what's been on your mind, that's why those nightmares, thinking you killed your own brother?' She put her head on Neil's shoulder and Neil took her hand.

'I was on the run for years until your father gave me a chance. But I always feared the law would catch up with me sooner or later. I didn't ask for your hand with that in my past.'

'Once I was out of jail, I set out to look for you. I figured you were one scared man. You were fox-sly, Neil. Every time I thought your trail was warm and getting hotter, it turned cold. You sure roamed far and wide. But somehow I sensed I was getting close when I rode into Arizona Territory after hunting eight years.'

In the midst of their revelations to each other, Joel Dunne rode up. He was dressed in his own clothes.

'I ain't never had a shot of whiskey,' Joel said, 'but I swore last night I was seeing double.' He scratched his head. 'Actually if it weren't for that scar on your brother's face, Neil, I would have been seeing double.' Joel set a small bundle on the table. 'I brought back your clothes, Neil, and I'm beholden to you.'

'You came just in time, Joel,' Merle chided. 'I'll set a plate for you for dinner.' She gave him a warm smile of welcome.

'Thank you, ma'am. You set a right good table. I could smell your cooking a mile away.' Joel turned to Neil. 'I ain't of age yet, not 21, so Doc Whitman arranged to be my guardian for the next three years. He said if anything happened to him maybe you'd take over. That's if it's no bother.'

'Joel, I'd be mighty proud to and honored.' He grinned. 'Joel you mightn't be nigh on to 21 yet but you *are* a man.'

At dinner, Neil and Phil related their stories again for the benefit of Joel. 'And that's the last time I'll spout mine,' Neil declared.

Joel added that he hoped to see a lot of Neil and Merle and Neil's brother in the future.

'I'm in my dad's home again and Uncle Caleb's is empty. I don't know where his cook went, but she's not there. The crew said they'd stick by me. No one working the mother lode at their mines will ever have cause to worry about the Gila.'

'Joel, I'll send Zack Meadows around to give you

a hand for awhile,' Neil said. 'That is, if you'd like me to.'

'I'd be obliged for sure.'

'You understand, Joel, why folks stayed away from your uncle's funeral,' Neil said. He didn't want it to sound like an apology.

'Yeah, but I felt I ought to be there even though he hated me.'

On Sunday morning, August 17th, Merle, Neil and Phil attended services at the little church in Apache Bend. A buzz went through the congregation when it spotted the twins together, but Gabriel Ashe frowned at the show of interest.

Merle and Neil were among the folks they knew best. Glancing around the pews, Neil spotted the smithy, Homer Breihalter, Eddie Cox, the owner of the Sagebrush Saloon; Frank Yegelstrom, the owner of the General Store; Sheriff Rengert;, Zack and Dolly Meadows; Lars and Ingrid Olsen; Harry and Millie Hawthorne; young Joel Dunne; Matt and Rebecca Felkins; the lame Brad Connors; Ken and Betsy Vanderman; Doc Whitman; Amy Gentian, the school ma'am; Ned Lockhart, Pete Sanford and Jim Naylor of the Benson crew; and in a far corner sat Thunder Cloud, looking uncomfortable in go-to-meeting clothes.

Most of the people in Apache Bend were now aware of the death of Caleb Dunne and of his mideeds that brought him shame. Still, Gabriel Ashe warned the little flock about the wages of sin. He pointed out the danger of trodding a sidewalk where the wooden boards were labeled deceit and avarice and envy and false witness.

Neil, though hearing the words, dwelt only upon

the fact that this was the first peaceful Sabbath he and Merle had enjoyed in weeks.

After the service, Neil and Merle stood before the congregation and announced that they were betrothed. The wedding would take place a month later, mid-September, and all were invited.

The small congregation forgot that it was in church and, to the apparent dismay of Parson Ashe, stood and cheered.

'If you want, I'll play my fiddle at your wedding,' Homer Breithalter offered. 'Won't take no fee neither, you hear?'

'This is a bright day for Apache Bend,' Doc Whitman told Neil and Merle once all were outside the church. 'I'm going to change my calendar to this year and mark this date. My Martha won't mind. Haven't been so proud since Sam Houston got Santa Anna by the tail, let me tell you.'

Neil grinned. 'You've told me a hundred times.'

Following Sunday dinner, Merle said she intended to ask Doc Whitman to give her away. 'And I want Amy Gentian for my bridesmaid.'

'And I'm asking my brother, Phil, to stand up with me.' Then, he clasped his twin on the shoulder. 'Now you know what just about everybody does in Apache Bend. I reckon I want to know what you aim to do, Phil. Go back to Georgia?'

'No. The South we knew, that we grew up in, ain't there any more. It's gone forever. No more dreams, no future there. 'I'm glad our mother and father aren't there to see it. The carpetbaggers, the destruction, the hunger and the darkies leaving, it would break their hearts, Neil.'

'We've got a mine to run here, Phil. there's work in the mines. It's good land, brother, Arizona Territory. It'll grow and prosper. Apache Bend'll have an increase in population, Ingrid Olsen's baby's gonna show up soon.'

Phil shook his head.

Neil pressed on. 'Joel Dunne will sure need a hand. So will Brad Connors since his foreman was killed. Apache Bend's a fine place to settle down.'

'With whom?' Phil asked. 'You're the lucky one, Neil. You've got Merle. Settle down? With whom?' he repeated.

Just then, the front door was pushed open and Amy Gentian, looking prettier than Neil could remember, stood in the doorway. No wonder the young bucks in Apache Bend pressed for her company.

'We're going to have another box social,' she announced, 'An All Hallow E'en, this time inside the school. You've got time to make costumes.'

Neil saw that his brother was staring at the school teacher as if he had never seen a girl before. Phil had stared like that at Amy Gentian in church this morning, too.

Amy's eyes brightened as she caught sight of Neil's twin. Neil thought, she can't take her eyes off Phil. Could it be …

'With that scar, Phil McAdam, you could come as a pirate.'

Phil grinned and nodded. 'Blame my brother for it.'

'You'll need to wear a special costume so I can tell you apart from Neil. You'll feel right at home in Apache Bend.'

Neil and Merle exchanged glances. then they

looked at Phil and Amy and smiled.

The answer to Phil's question, about whom he could settle down with, stood just an arm's length away